A Novel of Haiti
LAURA
ROSE
WAGNER

HOLD TIGHT DON'T LET GO

AMULET BOOKS
NEW YORK

A portion of the author's proceeds from the sale of this book goes to the Centre d'Education Spéciale (www.ceshaiti.org) and Ti Kay Haiti (www.tikayhaiti.org) to support their work providing education and healthcare in Haiti.

PUBLISHER'S NOTE: This is a work of fiction. Names, characters, places, and incidents are either the product of the author's imagination or are used fictitiously, and any resemblance to actual persons, living or dead, business establishments, events, or locales is entirely coincidental.

Library of Congress Cataloging-in-Publication Data

Wagner, Laura Rose.
Hold tight, don't let go / by Laura Rose Wagner.
pages cm
Summary: In the aftermath of the 2010 earthquake in Haiti, Nadine goes to live with her father in Miami while her cousin Magdalie, raised as her sister, remains behind in a refugee camp, dreaming of joining Nadine but wondering if she must accept that her life and future are in Port-au-Prince.
ISBN 978-1-4197-1204-3 (hardback)
1. Haiti Earthquake, Haiti, 2010—Juvenile fiction. [1. Haiti Earthquake, Haiti, 2010—Fiction. 2. Earthquakes—Fiction. 3. Cousins—Fiction. 4. Separation (Psychology)—Fiction. 5. Refugee camps—Fiction. 6. Port-au-Prince (Haiti)—Fiction. 7. Haiti—Fiction.] I. Title. II. Title: Hold tight, do not let go.
PZ7.1.W34Hol 2015
[Fic]—dc23
2014019622

Book design by Maria T. Middleton
Drawing on page 60 by Michlove St. Fleur. Used by permission.

Printed and bound in U.S.A.
10 9 8 7 6 5 4 3 2 1

115 West 18th Street
New York, NY 10011
www.abramsbooks.com

Liv sa a dedikase a Melise Rivien
6 janvyè 1964–12 janvyè 2010

"Lè m'mouri, m'pa p'fin ale nèt."
—Feliks Moriso-Lewa, "Testaman"

For Melise Rivien
January 6, 1964–January 12, 2010

"When I die, I will not really be gone."
—Félix Morisseau-Leroy, "Testament"

Kenbe fèm, pa lage.
Hold tight, don't let go.

(One way to say "good-bye"
in Haitian Creole)

JANUARY 12, 2010

WHEN IT BEGINS, I AM SHELLING PIGEON peas, pwa kongo, into a metal bowl under the almond tree in Madame Faustin's garden. I sit on the low wooden chair, my knees apart, the unshelled peas nestled in my old yellow skirt, so faded it's almost white. Pwa kongo for sauce. The thin layer of dirt the pods leave on my fingers feels sticky as I crack them. My mother, my manman, is inside, upstairs from where we sleep in the basement, cleaning for Mme Faustin, who has gone out to the bank. My sister, Nadine, is up the road at Jimmy Jean-Pierre's house, waiting for our soap opera to come on at five. Then, out of nowhere, groans a deep, furious noise, a deafening growl and then a terrible shaking. The sound and the shaking become one sensation—I can't separate the two—and the world collapses.

I am a rag doll throttled in a dog's mouth. The earth lurches back and forth and back again, and then it shudders in violent waves. I can't keep my balance, and I fall to my knees. I see the house fall.

I know I should be afraid, but I feel nothing but numbness. It is the end of the world, and I pray, Please, God, please, God, oh, God, please. And I know that this is when I will die, and I say to the universe: okay.

Everything explodes in white: a chalky cloud of cement powder engulfs me, engulfs the house, engulfs the entire city of Port-au-Prince. With a roar we are all swallowed. The house is gone. The city is gone. The world is no wider than I am. I can't see more than inches from my face. Then the sound of the people rising up in prayer and song—the furious, screaming gratitude of the just-saved. Jezi! Jezi! and Mèsi Seyè! Mèsi Seyè! Thank you, Lord! My knees are bleeding. The blood is warm. My bare toes flex, scrape the dust. Somehow, I am not dead. The pwa kongo are scattered around me.

Everyone I know is gone. Manman is dead. Nadine is dead. I am the only one left. I try to call Nadine's cell phone, over and over. I text her, but there is no signal.

I am too stunned to scream. Everything is severed. Nothing is real except the dust and the blood. I can't think in words. An eternity passes in minutes, and there are no words. I'm still on my knees, and I lean into the dirt, I put my head to the ground, I'm screaming in my blood, but I can't make a sound; my heart is too tight. Everything in me is clenched like a fist.

The white dust begins to settle, but the world is still shaking, or it feels like it's shaking, or I am shaking. Nothing is the shape it was. Nothing. Then I see her, appearing like a ghost. Nadine staggers up the street and is not dead. She looks lost, as if she doesn't know the neighborhood, doesn't know the world anymore. Her face and lips and hair are caked white with dust. "Where is Manman? Where is Manman?" she keeps saying, as though by asking the question, she might force the answer out of me, out of the universe.

The words stick in my dry throat and I start to cry without tears. I cannot tell Nadine what she must already know: that Manman is somewhere amid the jagged cement angles and the crumpled rebar of the house, the concrete ceiling fallen to the concrete floor, the doorway like a collapsed mouth exhaling dust into the darkening sky.

"Manman!" screams Nadine. Her voice is a child's voice. "Manman! Come here, Manman! Stop it! Come back to us, Manman!"

The ground trembles again. Nadine falls to her knees. I take off running toward the house.

"Manman! I'm coming, okay? Just wait. Wait for me."

Nothing is where it is supposed to be. I can't tell what is the ceiling or the floor. Doors are no longer doors, walls are no longer walls. I don't know how to begin to get in. "Wait for me, Manman," I say again.

Another aftershock hits, and the house sinks and settles. "Magdalie, don't!" Nadine cries. "Please. You can't do anything."

I push at the cement, I scratch at the crevices until my fingers bleed. I start to cry. "Please, wait, Manman." It is so heavy. I can't move it. Manman is under there.

"Nadine, bring me something. Anything. Do you see a shovel? What do you see?"

"Do you hear her?" calls Nadine, her voice filled with panic and desperate hope. "Can you hear her? Is she alive?"

"Bring me a shovel or a hammer or something!" I scream. I throw my weight against the unyielding cement. One time on TV, I saw a woman lift a car off her child. They say if you love someone enough, you can do anything, you can find superhuman strength. "Help me! Help me, Nadine. Jesus, help me!"

The ground beneath my feet shudders. The retaining wall be-

hind me collapses, one of the cinder blocks grazes the back of my head. The roof caves in completely with a slow, shattering groan and a billow of white dust.

"Manman!" I scream.

"Magdalie, stop it." Nadine is sobbing. "Please, you're going to die, too."

A hard, rough hand grips my upper arm. "Stop, Magdalie."

I blink. "Tonton Élie?" My uncle, Manman's youngest brother. I don't know where he's come from. I don't know how long it's been. His face is grim, chalky dust creased into every line on his forehead. "Manman's under there," I explain. "I have to find her."

I try to pull away, but he's gripping my arm so hard it hurts. "Stop, Magdalie. Go back to your sister."

"No! Manman's under there!"

"You're not strong enough. I'll find her. I'll get a hammer and I'll find her."

"Let me help you!"

"Go to your sister," orders Tonton Élie. "Go to Nadine and go out to the street, away from the buildings."

"But, Tonton—"

"Nadine needs you, you understand?"

"Wi. Yes, Tonton."

I go to Nadine then. She is shivering and she lays her head in my lap. We huddle together on the street. Night falls, and it is so cold. The street is full of people. A man we don't know gives us a sheet, and we cover ourselves with it and pull up our knees, and we drag a piece of dusty cardboard over that. The gravel from the road sticks to the blood oozing from my knees and the back of my head.

Nadine and I never let go of each other's hands. All night, the earth shakes, again and again, until we can't tell whether the shaking is in the earth or in our bones or in our heads. The next aftershock might be the end; the earth might crack open and swallow us whole. A woman in white prays, until slowly, inconceivably, the sun begins to come up over what remains of Port-au-Prince.

In the morning, Tonton Élie comes to us. He looks weary and sucked dry.

"Girls, go down to Delmas 18, to Tati Geraldine's house."

"What about Manman?" asks Nadine.

"I'm looking for her," says Tonton Élie.

"Is she dead," I say. It doesn't sound like a question at all.

"It'll be easier to look, now that it's light."

"Tonton . . ."

"Go to Tati Geraldine's house, Magda. You can't stay in the street."

"Can we go to your house, Tonton?"

"It fell, too, Magdalie. Flat." He turns around and goes back to the house.

Nadine reaches out and clasps my hand, and we go.

Nadine and I stumble through the ruins of the city. Our world has collapsed, the buildings crumbled inside out. Our everyday world is unfamiliar. Our school has buckled. Our church is cracked and tilted like a boat in the wind. We walk over the dead, and there is no space in my head to think about that. The streets are still full of people—injured people, stunned people, people seeking help, people trying to help others. So many of them are covered in white dust.

A woman, a mother, sits alone holding two tiny patent leather shoes, wiping the dust off them, polishing them against her skirt. Her eyes are dead. An older man keens, "My wife is gone, my wife is gone," and another man seizes him around the waist to keep him from falling down. But most people aren't screaming or crying. The city is simply . . . migrating. We are migrating. I am numbly surprised to see all these people because I thought maybe everyone in the world had died.

The sidewalks cannot hold all the bodies. Some are wrapped in sheets. I keep noticing small details: plastic pearl earrings, a necklace with a dolphin, a Boston Celtics T-shirt, a pair of jeans with rhinestones on the back pockets. Those people put on their clothes yesterday morning, pulling on their pants or skirts and shirts, fastening their bras and belts, not realizing those were the clothes they would die in. Some have on only one shoe. Their feet are callused from when they used to walk. A dead woman's skirt is tangled around her waist. A dead man's T-shirt rides up, showing the world the bottom of his fat gut. Everything and everyone is exposed.

I cry a little, but I can't really feel anything. Time doesn't exist anymore. There is no more future. I say, "Thank you, Jesus, thank you, Jesus, please, Jesus . . ." over and over. Words flow through my body, like blood or air, reminding me that I am still alive. Nadine and I cling to each other as if we are one person.

We make our way to the house of the old lady Manman calls Tati Geraldine, her countrywoman, whom she knows from where she grew up, in St. Juste. That night, we all sleep in the lakou, the yard, with the ducks. Someone hears on the radio that a tsunami is coming. Anything seems possible. People start to run. The whole neighborhood runs. Everyone runs. The injured limp, if they can. If they can't, people carry them. Nadine and I run, too. We don't know where we're running. I feel strangely calm. We are running through a dreamscape. Nothing is surprising anymore. There is nowhere to go. Nowhere is safe. We stop running when we are too tired, hungry, exhausted, resigned to continue. Nadine says, "If the sea rises, we won't have time to get anywhere, anyway, Magdalie. It's enough." And she sits on the ground. But no tsunami comes.

On Thursday, Tonton Élie comes and joins us at Tati Geraldine's. He tells us they have found Manman's body, on what was the second floor of the house. The wrought-iron terrace door fell on her. The basement—our little space where we lived—is fine, the walls not even cracked.

I see black. They tell me I suffered a kriz—that I fell to the ground, shaking uncontrollably, my jaw clenched. I wake up later, bruised and scraped, my head aching, my knees bleeding again, with Nadine lying next to me. She doesn't say anything, and she hardly ever speaks of Manman again.

Manman was ironing when she died. Hearing that made me angry. She always hated ironing.

At first everyone tries to find out who survived, and then, after a while, we start not wanting to know anymore. The city smells cloying, the wrong kind of sweet, the smell of rotting meat, of death. There are big blue flies everywhere, feasting. The smell sticks in the back of my throat, and I know that I will never stop tasting death.

On Friday, we move onto the local soccer field, me and Nadine and Tonton Élie. We are homeless. Mme Faustin's house is gone, and if Manman isn't cooking for her and washing her clothes, we have no right to live with her anyway. For two days we sleep on the ground. On the third day, we start building. We use what we find, sheets and sticks. We use what we salvage from the ruins. All around us, people are doing the same. Some we know, and some we don't. Now we know them. Everyone shares what they've got. No one is stingy. If someone cooks food over a small fire, everyone gets a little. Rice, spaghetti.

Now people talk, and they try to make sense of what happened.

They say the earthquake happened because we are all sinners, because we're all guilty of evil. Or they say it was a missile that France sent to kill us, or an underwater tunnel that the United States is building between Miami and Haiti. Me, I don't know why the earthquake happened. I don't understand it at all. I don't want to think it was random chance. But I can't force it to make sense, either. I don't want to believe that God would do this, and I don't want to believe that Satan is winning.

Now I know that there is nothing on this earth that cannot be ground to dust in seconds. Now I know I can't control anything at all. Everything I know is gone, everything, everything but Nadine. My sister, the only real thing left—the sound of her voice, the warmth and shape of her near me at night. She is as much of me as I am.

WHY WOULD I WRITE ABOUT IT, WHEN THERE is no way I could ever, ever forget?

It doesn't change anything if I write it down or not. It doesn't unbury anybody.

It doesn't save anyone.

I don't need to remember. I cannot forget.

There are memories you write down so you can preserve them. This isn't one of them.

There are memories you write down to get them out, to force them as far away from you as you can.

Only, it never works. My memories are out to get me. I push away the dog of memory with a stick as it gnashes its teeth and leaps for my throat. I remember, whether I want to or not.

I am only one witness, of millions. It doesn't matter what I say. It doesn't change a thing.

APRIL 2010

CHILDREN'S STORIES ARE SUPPOSED TO BEgin with *Once upon a time.* Once upon a time, I was an ordinary fifteen-year-old schoolgirl who lived with her manman and her sister in the downstairs part of a big cement house in Port-au-Prince, Haiti, which was owned by a lady named Madame Faustin. My aunt—who became my manman—raised me as her own child. I never knew any different. Manman was a servant in Mme Faustin's house, which meant she did all the cooking, the sweeping, the going-to-market, the washing, and everything else that needed to be done in that big house. Manman's work was hard, but she made a good life for my cousin and me. We laughed all the time—at Nadine's snoring, at goofy Tonton Bicha movies on our black-and-white TV, at Manman's jokes and stories from the countryside where she grew up. We'd make fun of the boys who whistled at us as we walked to school in the morning in our blue-and-white uniforms. We'd laugh in secret at Mme Faustin and her sour face and her middle-class airs, how she walked like a fat duck, and how she'd call for Manman to bring her her supper: "*Yo-LETTE!* Are you letting me starve tonight, Yolette?"

Life was boring and merciful then. Manman took care of everything. Looking at me and Nadine in those days, our skin soaped and rinsed and baby-powdered, our hair brushed and braided, our uniforms clean and ironed, nobody would ever know we were poor. "Your clothes are your passport," Manman always said as she made sure our socks came up to just the right place on our shins. Everything neat and in its place.

Now, for me and Nadine, that life, that world is gone.

Now it is me, Nadine, and Tonton Élie. He is not someone we would live with otherwise. The situation made us live together. He is our uncle, but we're not really used to him. He doesn't have children, and he doesn't know very much about teenage girls. He's a mechanic and an electrician. He spends his days looking for work or fixing up old secondhand radios and TVs. He mostly ignores us or gets impatient with us. So in a way, it's just me and Nadine.

We live in the camp down the road from the place Tonton Élie used to live, on the old soccer field that's been filled with people since January 12. Our house is not a tent (though there are tents around it—little red Coleman camping tents from the United States and huge white domes donated by one relief organization or other). But sometimes we call it "the tent." Actually, it's a house made of plywood, sheet metal, and plastic tarps. Tonton Élie built it himself, with Nadine's friend Jimmy and some other guys who live around here. They nailed the tarps to the plywood, through caps from old Prestige beer bottles and old Couronne soda bottles, the caps' serrated sides down. The bottle caps help keep the nails from tearing the plastic tarps when the wind blows.

We are still afraid of sleeping under cement roofs. Everybody is—everybody in this city is afraid of that. Everybody is ready to run all the time. When a water truck goes by, when a strong wind blows, when someone jiggles their foot against the table, and sometimes when there's nothing at all but we imagine the tremor in our heads—we run. We dream about earthquakes—in our nightmares we are frozen and cannot run. This kid Kervens who lives in the tent near the mapou tree, he was under the rubble for seven hours on January 12, and now he won't sleep without his sneakers on his feet.

At least in the camp we don't have to worry about being crushed if our tents fall.

Nadine and I share a bed, as we always have, and Tonton Élie makes his bed of blankets on the floor every night. He grumbles that his body is too old for this. He isn't more than thirty, though, so his body is just fine. We've got electricity whenever the government turns it on. Tonton Élie set up our tent and a bunch of the tents around us with a web of wires reaching up to the electrical pole, which isn't technically legal, but the police have other things to worry about. As long as the electricity is on, we can charge our phones and watch TV.

As far as camps go, ours is medium-size, maybe fifty tents. It is not huge like the one on the Champ de Mars or La Piste, but it's not tiny and hidden on some hillside, either. That is good, says Tonton Élie; it is good to be visible and near the road, because it means relief organizations will see us and give us aid. He says that's the way it's going to be now, and there's nothing shameful about it, it's not the same as begging because the country is broken, and everyone will come and help us.

Right after the earthquake, when the whole country was upside-down, we got a little bit of food from the organizations. Tonton Élie had me and Nadine stand in line because the organizations said women and girls first, women and girls are more trustworthy, women and girls won't push and shove like men will. So we stood in line for hours and hours and hours, sweating in the sun with hundreds of other people, and all we got was two cans of oil and a little bit of dried rice and beans for all that trouble. Tonton Élie said that was a scam; he'd never make us wait in line like that again.

A big tanker truck comes and delivers water to the camp twice a week, pumping it into huge yellow rubber bags that sit in the sun, getting hot. Even though the organizations say it's good potable water, nobody believes them. The water tastes funny, like the rubber it sits in. So we use it for washing and maybe for cooking, but definitely not for drinking. We buy little bags of treated water to drink, or if we've really got no money, we collect rainwater off the tarp and boil it.

We don't go to school anymore, even though the schools reopened this month. The president says it's time for life to start again, but Nadine and I don't have anyone to pay for school since Manman died. Tonton Élie can't afford it. We don't do much of anything but wait. Living in a camp is all about waiting—for food, for water, for something to change. Of course, it is also hard. But it's hard in a drudging, dragging way. We are fighting for our survival, but the fight is tedious and slow-motion.

When we are bored, Nadine and I practice cosmetology on each other. We've been doing each other's hair since we were little girls, but now we're moving on to other things: manicures and pedicures, acrylic fingernails, makeup, eyebrows. I wasn't nervous when I let Nadine go at my eyebrows with a Gillette, because even if she made a mistake, there's no one else to see or care.

Yesterday afternoon, I tried putting acrylic nails on Nadou. I pressed them down with Krazy Glue and then cut them, just like our neighbor Jilène does when she gives manicures and pedicures under the mapou tree in the camp, but they were still long, like talons.

"It kind of hurts, Magda," Nadine told me.

"You'll get used to it, Nadou," I said.

I have a lot of nail polishes, though some of them are old now, sticky and thick or almost used up. Some of them were ours from before the earthquake, and they got dug out of the rubble. Some of them Jilène gave me. She is nice to us because we have no mother. When you put all the nail-polish bottles together, it's a lot of colors.

I tried drawing designs on Nadou's acrylic claws. Squiggles, swirls, a rainbow, flowers, a butterfly.

Nadou peered down at her thumb. "Is that a spider?"

"It's a rose."

"It sort of looks like a spider."

"It has a *stem*."

Some nails turned out better than others. The best nail was probably the green one with gold sparkles and a black tip.

"My fingers feel really heavy," said Nadou.

"You'll get used to it," I said again, with confidence.

"How will I wash the dishes?" she asked.

"Haven't you seen women with acrylics doing all kinds of things? They wash dishes. They wash clothes. They type. They cook. They just get used to it."

Nadine thought for a moment. "How will I wipe myself?"

She has given up on her new look after only a day, after wincing every time she accidentally hit her hands against anything and sleeping last night without moving, her fingers spread out carefully on the sheet. Now she comes to me today, saying, "Magda, we've got to get these off me."

"Really? You should try them for another day."

"I *can't*. I can't do anything. Unless you want to do all the cooking and all the cleaning yourself?"

"Fine."

I heat a little water in an old can over the charcoal. "You're supposed to soak your hands in warm water, and they'll pull right off," I assure her.

"Hmm!" she says, but she places her fingertips in the water.

I tug gently on the purple flower on Nadou's right index finger.

"It seems stuck," she observes.

"Just a little harder," I promise, and I yank.

"*Mezanmi!*" she cries. "Oh my God! No, no, no. It's not working. Don't do that again."

"It's totally getting loose. Absolutely. I just need something to help pry it off. Wait a second." I rummage through my cosmetics kit until I find a nail file and an old pair of pliers of Tonton Élie's.

"Magdalie, you're going to kill me!"

"No, no, I know what I'm doing." I jam the file between the acrylic and Nadine's real nail, scraping at the glue, which comes away as a flaky white powder.

"That's my own nail coming off!" whines Nadine.

"That's the glue, dummy. I've got it under control."

Once I've gotten the nail a little loose, I grab the tip with the pliers. "It's going to slide right off now," I announce, and I twist.

"*Anmwèeeeeey!* Heeeeelp!" yells Nadou as she pulls her hand away from me and turns toward the wall. Actual tears glisten in her eyes.

"I guess you've just got sensitive fingertips, ti douyèt, you fragile thing," I tell her.

"You're not my friend!" Nadine mutters, wiping her eyes. "I hate you!"

"You know, I'm going to go borrow some of Tonton Élie's paint thinner," I decide.

When I return, we prop open the front door of the tarp-house and tie up the lace curtain to let the fumes escape, and Nadou grudgingly places her fingertips in the bowl of thinner. ("This is your fault, Magda," she hisses.) A thick band of sunlight splashes across the inside of our home: the swept-dirt floor, the battered suitcases full of clothes, Tonton Élie's half-fixed circuit boards, and a huge wall calendar, distributed by Prestige beer, featuring two women in bikinis on a beach. All the noise of the camp flows into our private world: the revving of motorcycle taxis, the bleating of goats, the squalling of babies, the sound of a woman washing her clothes and singing an evangelical hymn.

"Keep soaking them," I tell Nadou.

"Hmmph!" she says.

Eventually, after some scraping, paring, and pulling, we get the nails off, though Nadine yells and writhes as though I were pulling out her teeth instead.

"I think my nails are only half as thick as they used to be," she moans, sticking her hands under her arms protectively.

"It's really a pity I had to break the acrylics," I say, ignoring her. "Some of the designs were really beautiful."

"You'll have to do it again sometime," replies Nadine flatly.

People used to call Nadine and me the marasa, the twins, because we are so close in age and look so much alike. Not the bad kind of marasa, who hate each other from the womb and can kill each other with a curse without even trying, but the good kind, who are better and more powerful for being together. They said we looked like two drops of water. Same color skin, same eyes, same gap in our front teeth. People said our names as if they were one word strung together: *Magdalie-and-Nadine* or sometimes *Nadine-and-Magdalie.* But we aren't twins, we aren't even sisters. Nadine is my cousin. She was born in Port-au-Prince and is an only child. I was born on a mountain a day's walk from the town of Jérémie on Haiti's southwest tip. I came to live with Nadou and Manman when I was three, when my own mother, Manman's younger sister, died while giving birth to my little brother, who died, too.

My father was a good man who loved me, but he was poor. They tell me he had lots of breadfruit trees and yams, but he had no money to send me to school, and so he sent me to the capital instead. A few years after I was born, he died suddenly, with blood coming out of his mouth. Manman said it was a maladi mistik, a disease that somebody had cursed him with. And that is the story of how I became Yolette's second daughter. As long as I can remember, I called her Manman.

No one knows me like Nadine does, and no one knows Nadine like I do. In truth, we are marasa not because we're identical, because we really aren't, but because we complete each other, like two halves of a whole. I am louder than she is, and I'm not good at hiding things or keeping secrets—especially my own. Nadou is quieter and more closed up. Manman and I used to say we were the only people who knew what

Nadine was thinking. Nadine liked to joke, "Bon, why do I need to talk when you talk enough for both of us, Magda? You run your mouth too much!" But it's not that she doesn't talk at all. Nadine talks to me, because I am her confidante, and her sister, and her true and forever friend.

Before the quake, we all lived at Mme Faustin's: Manman, Nadine, and me. Manman never made enough money to finish the house she had tried to build in Port-au-Prince, and Mme Faustin's was in a better neighborhood anyway. "I can't just let you girls loose on the street so men can talk to you whenever they want and have their way with you. I can't let you grow up in the slums. You understand?"

"Wi, Manman," Nadou would say, then giggle.

"Little innocent," Manman would grumble. "Ungrateful. Oh, I break my body for you, pitit!" But she'd laugh, too, and slap Nadou on the behind.

Sometimes Nadine was embarrassed by Manman's lack of education, because she was both a Catholic who went to church and a vodouyizan who got mounted by the spirits, the lwa.

"That's backwards belief, devil stuff," she would say.

"If you don't believe in vodou," I would ask her, "then why are you so afraid of it?"

Manman was serious about the spirits, but she laughed about it, too. Ask her what she believed and she'd start shaking and jiggling her whole body, making fun of people who get mounted by the lwa, even though she did, too. Manman believed in vodou, and she believed in the

Church. She believed in healing plants and she believed in antibiotics. Manman could believe in everything. She had a lot of faith.

Even though Manman didn't have any formal education, she was clever. She used nearly every gourde she earned to send us both to Catholic school, because she knew it was better than the little neighborhood school. When I was little, I figured out that I liked to read and write, and the nuns would sometimes lend me extra books to read at home. I'd sit on the low wooden chair near Manman while she cooked over the charcoal fire, and I'd read stories to her, because she loved stories but she'd never learned to read. When I ran out of borrowed stories, I began to write my own for her. She said my stories were better than the radio, better, even, than the soap operas.

"Pitit!" she'd say. "Child! Where did you learn to do that?"

I wish I had memorized Manman's face, and her hands—the burns, the scars, the calluses. Her hands were always warm. She used to rub my back with palma christi oil when I was sore from carrying my backpack, and she'd sing us lullabies about the demons that hide in the dark wilderness, the things that would eat us up if given a chance. When she braided our hair, she'd scratch the teeth of the plastic comb against our scalps to loosen the dandruff, and it was the sweetest relief—I loved getting my hair braided, just for that feeling. When Nadine and I were little girls, we'd pat too much talcum on our necks, and Manman would look at us covered in white dust, and exclaim, "Oh, look how well these little fish are covered in flour! We'll fry them up tonight!"

Manman loved to laugh! I always remind myself of that, of how often she used to laugh and tell jokes. Sometimes the jokes were about sex and especially men's zozos, which embarrassed Nadine more than they embarrassed me.

"You've never seen the old tonton who sells cigarettes with his thing all swollen from—what's that disease that can make your foot swell up like an elephant's?"

"Filariasis, Manman," I'd say.

"Fil-a-ri-a-sis," she'd repeat carefully. "And his thing is swelled up as big around as his leg, poor guy . . . But can you imagine? He'd tear up any woman he tried to sleep with!"

Nadou would squeal, "Man*man!*" and hide her face in her hands.

Even though these memories make me feel closer to Manman, I can't talk about them at all with Nadine. She gets too upset. She never talks about Manman; she just cries when she thinks no one is looking. Me, I don't care who sees me cry. I cry easily, out in the open. Nadou shakes her head and tells me, "Hold on to yourself, Magda!" But I don't want the day to come when I stop crying for Manman.

Now we are surrounded by things pulled out of the rubble of our home. Some of our clothes, our photos, even our talcum powder and nail polish. Our old geography books. Nadou's *High School Musical* poster. My journal. It doesn't make any sense to me, still, that all these things—things that Manman once touched with her hands or wore on her body—have outlived her. She is not here, but all these things she touched are still here. And we are still here, and we must take care of each other as she took care of us.

JULY 2010

NADOU'S PAPA IN MIAMI HAS BEEN TALKING about bringing her there. He has a lawyer, but the process is very long and complicated. Tonton Élie has to keep taking Nadou to appointments at the US embassy and all these other places. We don't know when she'll get her visa or even if she'll get it. Nadou keeps her phone right next to her all the time, even when she's bathing, just in case her papa calls.

I tell her, "If you drown your phone in the kivèt, he'll never be able to call you again."

Nadine's papa is not family to me, so he can't do anything for me. But Nadou promises that if she goes to America, I will go, too. "You're my sister," she tells me. "Even if we can't leave at the same time, I'll send for you as soon as I can."

Nadou and I dream about Miami and all the things

we will do once we are there together. Our dreams get bigger and bigger, more exaggerated—we keep trying to come up with something bigger and better than the last time.

"We could go bowling," I say. "Like in Justin Bieber's 'Baby' video."

"We could see a movie in a theater," Nadou says. "On a big screen."

"We could get our belly buttons pierced."

"We could do that *here.*"

"We could get air-conditioning."

"It might be *cold* there."

"We could make money and buy a car and drive it all the way to New York City," I say.

"All the way to Montreal," Nadou says.

"All the way to Paris." I giggle.

"We could get real jobs."

"We could work at a supermarket. Or a mall."

"We could go to college."

"We could become doctors."

"We could become president!"

"Of Haiti or of the United States?"

"Both!"

We laugh like it's a big joke, because joking is the only way we have to talk about things we can't really control.

I DON'T KNOW WHAT NADINE ATE THAT I didn't eat yesterday. We had mayi moulen with sòs pwa, cornmeal with bean sauce, for dinner, which we cooked together while Tonton Élie was out listening to politics on the radio and drinking kleren somewhere with other men. And I was feeling fine. Then, in the middle of the night tonight, Nadine shakes me awake.

"Magda!" she hisses.

I sit up, startled, my heart pounding. "What!"

"Twalèt kenbe m!" she whispers. "I have to go to the bathroom! *Now!*"

I flop back down and turn over, pulling the sheet over my head. "Can't you hold it until morning? Tonton Élie isn't back yet. You know we're not supposed to leave the tent at night without him."

"No!" Nadine squeaks more loudly. "I need to go *now*."

"Nadou, it's the middle of the night—"

"Do you want me to have diarrhea in this bed?"

I shine the display of my cell phone over Nadine. She definitely looks uncomfortable, with a light sheen of sweat at her hairline. "Fine, let's go," I mumble, and I slip on my plastic sandals.

"This is all your fault," she hisses accusatorially as she unbolts the sheet of plywood that makes up our front door, her fingers slipping as she rushes. "I knew you would put too much clove in the sòs pwa. You're *always* adding too many cloves. You *know* it does this to me."

"I added no more clove than anyone else would have." *As much as Manman taught me to add,* I think to myself.

Using my cell phone as a flashlight, we wend our way to the camp toilets. They are portable plastic toilets, and one of the aid organizations pays people who live in the camp a little bit of money to clean them. This is how shameful our lives have become: foreigners paying us to clean our own houses. The toilets are hot and horrible and make me gag. There is always something leaking and creeping across the sidewalk, a slow-moving puddle that trickles into the street. They don't even have doors anymore—people took them to use the wood for other things—so you'd never use one alone. You need someone with you to stand in the open doorway, and, anyway, it doesn't feel safe to be there alone, especially at night.

Nadine and I have trained ourselves never to have to use the camp toilets if we can help it. When we have to pee, we go in a plastic kivèt, then pour it into the sewage ditch and rinse it out: easy. When we've got to do more than that, we have to strategize. I mean, it really changes things when you have to plan. It means I don't drink coffee anymore.

Most of the time, Nadine will go to her friend Jimmy Jean-Pierre's place, which is just a couple of blocks away, where they have a real toilet. She keeps her own roll of toilet paper on top of our TV and takes it with her whenever she goes. She says Jimmy wouldn't have a problem with my doing that, too, but I don't know him that well, and I'm embarrassed, and I don't want his family to think I'm a freeloader. Sometimes I go to the latrine behind the little restaurant across the street, which is owned by a lady named Loulouze who wears huge earrings. "Of course, my child, you've got no mother. Use it whenever you like." But I don't want to take advantage of her kindness.

And you can't always plan ahead . . .

In the dark, on nights when we don't have power, the camp looks like a different place than it does in the day, deserted and menacing. Even my fears are blurry—the bogeymen of my childhood imagination, and the rapists Tonton Élie is always warning us of. A lone streetlight, installed by a relief organization, illuminates the area right around the toilets, but until we reach it, we are in a landscape of invisible phantoms and lurking monsters.

"Go faster, go faster!" Nadine begs.

She takes a deep breath, then hurries inside and pulls down her pajama pants just in time. I stand where the door should be, blocking the view of all the nonexistent passersby, and I pick at a hangnail, trying not to listen to what Nadine is doing.

I hold my breath. This is one of the worst smells in the world. I can think of only one smell that's worse, and that's the stench of rot that rose up from the city in the days after the quake, that told you death was everywhere, everywhere. But the toilet smell is terrible in a different way, maybe because we're supposed to get used to it. I keep holding my breath, and my chest gets tighter and tighter. The air from my lungs backs up into my throat, my nose, my mouth, and I try to release it bit by bit without breathing any new air in. It takes more than a minute for me to feel dizzy and see purple-black spots, and without thinking, I gulp in a huge quaff of warm, putrid air.

It is acrid and horrible, searing and thick with shit and poison. I imagine the germs buzzing in the air, traveling down into my lungs. The smell is so strong, it lingers on my tongue. My stomach lurches, and I feel a sour burn at the back of my throat.

"Nadou, are you finished?"

"I'm not sure . . . ," she whimpers miserably. "I think there might still be more in there . . ."

I am brisk with Nadine because sometimes she can get very exaggerated about illness and discomfort—she has *always* been this way—and because I would rather be sleeping peacefully in bed than standing out in the middle of the camp in the middle of the night, my cheap plastic sandals sticking in the filthy toilet mud, holding my breath outside this sickening cesspool. Still, I'm glad

I am here. It is unpleasant to be sick, but it would be so much worse to be sick alone in this place. I feel sad and lonely just imagining Nadou stumbling through the dark alone, by the dim light of the cell phone, to have diarrhea in the horrible camp toilet. Who would block the doorway for her if I wasn't there? Who would block the doorway for me, if our roles were reversed? Who would be there to laugh about it with me afterward, to laugh at the stupidity and awfulness of it all?

"Okay, let's go," says Nadine. Her voice sounds small. "My butt's all raw," she whispers with a trace of an apologetic smile on her face.

"Anmwèy!" I burst out laughing and gasp, "Mezanmi, Nadou!"

We walk more slowly back to our now-home as the first pink fingers of light appear over the horizon and the camp's roosters rouse themselves and begin to crow.

SEPTEMBER 2010

NADOU'S PAPA CALLED FROM MIAMI YESterday evening and told her, "I got it, pitit mwen. I got the visa." I was bathing in Loulouze's yard—the lady with the big earrings, who says a young girl should have privacy to wash her chouchoun—and when I came back to the tent, Nadou's face was blank. I thought something terrible had happened. I thought someone had died.

"Nadou, what's wrong? What happened?"

She couldn't look at me. She was looking somewhere over my shoulder, and she said, "He got it. He got it. I'm going. I'm supposed to go to the US consulate tomorrow and pick up all the documents."

It took a minute for me to even move. Then I grabbed her hands in mine and held them tight. "That's great! Finally! That's fantastic news!" My voice was brittle with enthusiasm. I was pretending, for Nadou's sake. I knew she could tell the difference. But there was no point in throwing myself to the ground and screaming, "Don't go, don't go!" Of course she must go. Anybody, given the chance, would go, would leave this broken city.

Nadine shivered. "We'll figure out a way for you to come. I don't know how, but we'll do it, okay?"

"Yeah. I know. We can do it. Nadou, stop looking so sad. Stop it! Be happy instead."

"You promise you'll come?" she asked me.

"Of *course*. Stop being dumb."

"Tomorrow we'll start figuring it out," Nadine decided. "After I get back from the consulate. We'll start doing research. I'll ask Jimmy. His dad's in Miami. And he's good at computers. He'll know."

"Okay. Agreed. I promise."

"I know, sista."

Nadou spent almost all day waiting in line at the US consulate, so we're only just now going to meet up with Jimmy at the cybercafe, at five P.M. She came home looking exhausted, clutching a fat manila envelope to her chest. DO NOT OPEN UNTIL AT UNITED STATES IMMIGRATION, it says. It is sealed with thick, clear tape. On the front is a grainy black-and-white photograph of an unsmiling, serious Nadou. Underneath is all the information they need about her: her birthdate (July 28, 1994), her place of birth (Port-au-Prince, Haiti), her father's name (Duverlus, Frantz) and status (US Resident), and her mother's name (Étienne, Yolette) and status (deceased).

"How did it go?" I ask.

"There were *so* many people there," says Nadine, her eyes glassy. "Standing in line, all day. All around the block. Under the hot sun, all day." She shakes her head in wonder. "So many people. Most of them weren't approved; they weren't there to pick anything up. They were just . . . just waiting and hoping."

"Just think, if all those people had real jobs . . . ," I say. "Just think of where this country might be."

Nadine tears open a bag of drinking water with her teeth and sucks it down. "That *is* their job. Trying to get out." She tosses the plastic bag into the drainage ditch a few feet from our front door. "Let me call Jimmy and tell him we're on our way."

The cybercafe is packed at this time of day, mostly with high school and university students who have gotten out of school and have come to chat online, send e-mail, or do homework. A young man in a corner is on an international call, speaking English loudly. I can't tell whether he's good at it or not, but he sounds frustrated. In another corner, a staticky TV is playing a Whirlpool commercial with an adorable little light-skinned girl and her handsome light-skinned father and their beautiful kitchen full of shiny new appliances. The world in that commercial isn't meant for people like me, but I can't help humming along to the Whirlpool song.

Jimmy gives me a kiss on the cheek in greeting, then wraps his arm around Nadou's waist and pulls her close to him. Jimmy has always liked Nadine. They SMS all the time, and I always know when she's gotten a message from him, because she has a special ringtone for him—Celine Dion's *"Je lui dirai."* He wants to be her boyfriend, and she's kissed him a few times, but she decided it would be better to just be friends.

"Let's go see what we can find." Jimmy pulls a chair up to one of the computers. Nadou sits in a chair next to him, and I lean over her shoulder to watch.

"Your chin is pointy," she says.

"Your shoulder is bony."

Jimmy starts typing without even looking at the keyboard. His fingers are slim and elegant. He smells like cologne.

"First you go to yahoo-dot-fr," he explains. "Then type in 'tickets port-au-prince miami.'" He pushes the keyboard toward Nadine, who slowly begins to peck out the words, using two fingers. "You're going to have to get good at computers when you're living in America," he counsels her. "Now click on Search."

The computer burbles electronically, and then a site comes up that lists a bunch of airfares. I'm afraid to look—what if the ticket price is huge, so huge and expensive that I'll never be able to dream of buying one?

"Magda," says Nadine softly. I realize I've actually shut my eyes. "It's not *too* bad. Look."

They're all between $200 and $250 US for a one-way flight. I exhale. I start calculating it into gourdes . . . Around 10,000 gourdes. It's more money than I've ever seen. But it's not an *unimaginable* amount of money. It's not impossible.

"It shouldn't be hard, girls," Jimmy says assuredly. "The hard part will be the paperwork. Tonton Sam doesn't like Haitians coming in."

"Who's Tonton Sam?" I ask, confused. "Does he work at the airport?" I imagine a big fat man checking all the passports and turning Haitians away.

"It means America, Magdalie," explains Jimmy. "Uncle Sam. America doesn't like Haitians."

"Oh." I don't know what to say to that. I feel guilty, and I don't know why. "I knew that already."

"So it's not just buying your ticket. You have to get a visa and everything, like Nadine did."

"I can do it! I'll do it," Nadine declares. "I can get it for her."

Jimmy looks at Nadine as though she is stupid, but he doesn't say anything, because he likes her. All he says is, "I gotta go, little ladies. I have an exam in two days."

"*Mèsi,* Jimmy," says Nadine. "Thanks. You're so nice to me."

"I'll text you," he tells her. "Tonight."

"Ten thousand gourdes," I say to Nadine as we walk home through the smoky dusk. I repeat, "Ten thousand gourdes." I sing it softly, like a chant. The air smells like burning trash.

"We can do it," she says excitedly. "I'll be working on the visa from Miami, okay? I'll be able to do it, because I'll be a rezidan."

"Wi," I agree.

"And, Magda, you can be working on getting the money for the ticket."

"How? How will I do that?"

Nadine chews her bottom lip. "Like when Tonton Élie gets a job, you can ask him for money."

"No, I can't."

"Well . . . when he gives you money and sends you to the market to buy food, just keep a little of it. Bargain with the machanns as low as they'll go, and then keep a little, and tell Tonton Élie that they're selling whatever it is for twenty-five gourdes instead of twenty apiece."

I'm shocked. "You want me to steal from Tonton Élie, Nadou?"

Nadine slaps her hands together, fingers to palms, fingers to palms, and shrugs. "We have to do what it takes."

"Yeah."

"Or you could get a job."

"Yeah."

"I promise you, sista, I'm going to do whatever it takes."

And Nadine holds the promise out before me, and possibility shines in her eyes, as if her eyes contain both of our futures, and all I have to do is follow. None of this will be that hard. Nothing is impossible, with patience and faith. *Little by little, the bird builds its nest,* I remember Manman used to say.

NOVEMBER 2010

THIS MORNING NADINE WAKES UP AT FOUR to get ready. Her fingernails and toenails are painted red, and her hair is in curlers, after a trip to the beauty salon yesterday, and she's laid out the new outfit she got downtown—tight, skinny blue jeans, a white blouse, and a long vest that's the same golden-brown color as her strappy sandals. All new, not secondhand. Her earrings and necklace are gold-colored. Élie gave her all the money he got from cash-for-work, even if it means we'll be eating white-flour porridge for the next week. Looking at her, you wouldn't know she is poor. We are happy for her.

If Nadou can leave, that is good for her, maybe good for all of us.

Nadine is bathing, using the blue plastic kivèt. She stands behind the tent with a rigged-up tarp for cover, soaping herself up in her underpants. Around her, a couple of chickens cluck and dash out of the way when the water she pours over herself splashes them. Chickens are dumb. I am a few feet away, cooking over the charcoal: boiled plantains, fried chicken, and sauce made of onions, tomato paste, green onion, garlic, thyme, and a Maggi cube. It is early, but I want to make a good last meal for her, something that will sustain her until she gets to Miami. As she washes, I think, *This is the last time you'll have to bathe in cold water.*

She wraps herself in a towel and goes back inside the tent, to the clothes she's laid out on the bed we share. Nadine has always laughed at how I sleep "ugly," kicking my legs out and flinging my arms wide, reaching over and stealing her sheet in the middle of the night or waking her up by resting my head on her shoulder. I realize I will sleep alone from now on. For a second my life spins out of focus. I can't think about these things. My eyes sting. The chicken sizzles in the pot before me.

"Magda!" Nadine calls from inside. Her voice sounds like a child's. "Come help me do my hair!"

We learned to braid hair on each other as little girls, armed with cloth ribbons and plastic barrettes, and later we learned how to do perms on each other. This morning I take out Nadine's curlers and brush her hair, adding touches of pomade here and there. Nadine watches in a handheld mirror. She is so silent this morning. I feel the minutes rushing toward us.

"How do you feel?" I ask her.

Nadine pauses. "Bizarre."

Nadou hasn't seen her papa since he left, when she was, maybe, eight. He was never there for her; he just sent Manman a Western Union money transfer every once in a while. Nadine's father never mattered before, but now he matters more than anything. She has papers that say her father is a US resident, and her mother died in the earthquake, and because of these things Nadine has a visa to go to America forever.

That is the funny thing—Nadine and I are so much like sisters that we forgot we aren't really sisters. Until now. Before this, it never mattered. I was Manman's daughter. I'm still Manman's daughter, in every way but the one that matters now. It took months of appointments and DNA tests (taking her blood, scraping the inside of her cheek), but now Nadine has a passport and that thick, magical manila envelope sealed by the US consulate. It is her passage to lòt bò dlo, the other side of the water.

Nadine only picks at the chicken and banann bouyi I've set in front of her. She's too nervous, too busy fussing with her makeup and her clothes. I sit on the bed, still wearing the same T-shirt and skirt I slept in, watching her, trying to memorize her. She's already slipping away; she's halfway gone. *This separation is temporary,* I keep telling myself.

Since January 12, every good-bye feels like it might be forever.

Jimmy has come to see her off. He has a camera in his hand. He smiles.

"Come, Magdalie, let's take a photo," says Nadine,

and she tries to put her arm around me, but as soon as she does that, I start weeping.

"Don't hug me, or I'll cry," I tell her.

Jimmy snaps the photo and shows it to us. We look stupid—Nadine's arm wide open, failing to pull me in, her mouth in the middle of forming a word; me, still in my sleeping clothes, head down, a blur.

"Erase it," I tell Jimmy.

"But this is the last photo," he tells us.

I ask myself in my heart if I am jealous. God says we should not be envious of others, that it is a sin, but I still have to ask myself if, honestly, I am jealous of Nadine. She is leaving. She is going to a better place—to a place I have only seen in photos and in films, to a place where everyone has money, everyone has a car and a lawn and a flush toilet, where the streets are straight and flat and clean. To a place where she will go to university, and she can have a good life, where it will be easy to accomplish whatever she sets her mind to. To a place with no rubble and no makeshift tents. To a place without fear. I don't know when I'll join her. Maybe I am *supposed* to feel jealous. I ask myself and ask myself, I search the darkest places in my heart, but the truth is, I don't feel jealous at all. I just feel sad.

I'd wanted to give her something. I'd wanted to write her a poem or a story. I'd tried to write, but I couldn't think of what to say. Everything felt too heavy. I used to write all the time. I'd write about things I saw that day and about things I'd imagined, like romantic love, or stories in which the hardworking triumph and those who seek only pleasure are punished, tales with happy endings. I didn't realize it at the time, but they were a little like the soap operas Manman loved so much. I can't write those stories now. I can't write anything now.

Tonton Élie takes Nadine in his arms, which is awkward, because he's not normally affectionate. It just makes this day feel stranger and more uncomfortable. Élie can't go to the airport with us. He has to go break up rubble for that cash-for-work program the aid organizations run. If he doesn't go, they'll give his spot to someone else. "You are going to a better place," he tells Nadou. "Don't forget us. Don't forget your country. You are going to a more beautiful place so that you can come back someday and work to make things more beautiful here."

Nadine doesn't say anything, only sniffles. "Dakò," she finally whispers. "Okay."

I slip away to bathe quickly and get dressed before Jimmy gives us a ride to the airport. Jimmy's papa is lòt bò and sends him money every month. I put on one of our shirts, a yellow sleeveless blouse—we share all our clothes. Nadine has left almost all of them for me, and so now this is *my* shirt, not ours.

I keep thinking I can hold time still if I just concentrate on it.

We ride in silence to the airport, both of us in the backseat, holding hands. I think I should say something.

"Are you afraid of the airplane?"

"A little."

I can't think of anything else to say. Or maybe there

are so many things to say, but none of them come to the surface. I watch all the streets we know and try to imagine what it would be like to be seeing them for the last time. It is Saturday morning. Children gather around a broken water pipe on the side of a muddy street and fill their buckets. A woman with fat, grandmotherly arms sells ripe bananas, peanut butter, bread, and hard-boiled eggs out of a basket in front of one of the camps. A motorcycle taxi shoots by carrying a woman passenger sitting sideways, elegantly, not creasing her skirt. A banner across the road advertises a Médecins Sans Frontières clinic. An elaborate taptap bus painted with the face of Brazilian soccer star Kaka stops in front of us. For a moment I want to say: *Nadine, hold on to all this. Remember this. Not because it is all beautiful or good—so much of it is ugly and broken—but because it is ours.*

Nadine looks out the window, absorbed in thought, her eyes fixed on a future I cannot see. The road leading to the airport, past the Trois Mains statue, is also a camp. Over the clustered sunbaked tents, the blue and gray sea of tarps, rise billboards. One, for Delta Airlines, shows New York City and the Statue of Liberty looming over it. The billboard hangs over the camp like a question mark and a promise and a joke. I wonder if Nadine will get to go to New York City.

We arrive. Standing on the curb in front of the departure terminal with her small black suitcase, Nadine looks lost. She gazes at me with the same lost expression she had on January 12, when she cried out, "Where is Manman?" Now she pushes her phone into my hand—with the little pink sticker of a rose on it, with her special love-song ringtones, with the sudoku she used to play when she couldn't fall asleep. "I won't be able to use this," she says, and she clears her throat.

"Orevwa," I say. "Till we meet again, sista. Do well for yourself."

"Orevwa," says Nadine. "I'll miss you."

"We'll see each other very soon," I say firmly.

"Mwen pap janm lage w. I'll never let you go." She nods. "I'll get you to the US as soon as I can, as soon as I can."

We hug for a quick moment. I slip her fifty gourdes I've saved, in case she gets hungry. I thought there would be more to say.

I walk her as far as I can and then watch her join the line of passengers waiting to board their planes. My fingernails dig crescent moons into my palms. I watch the back of her head as she blends into the crowd, as she becomes just another person departing, as she disappears from my life.

DECEMBER 2010

MY LIFE IS STRANGE TO ME NOW. IT IS NOT my life. Manman is gone. Nadou is gone. Everyone and everything I was used to is gone. All the ordinary things I do are different now. I go through the routines of the day feeling like an actress in a TV drama. *Now she walks down the street alone to buy Maggi and parsley, fifteen gourdes in her hand*... The water bucket never felt so heavy when I walked with Nadine to fill it. We'd wait in line together for water and help each other hoist the buckets onto our heads so we wouldn't spill, and we'd gossip or sing all the way home. I had expected that life without Nadine would hurt, but I wasn't prepared for how boring it would be.

I can't wait until she sends for me.

Now I am the only one left to carry the water, to cook our food, to wash the clothes, to mop and sweep.

Sometimes it's just me and Tonton Élie, but most of the time there are other people staying with us or eating with us—cousins or neighbors from the country who come to town with a sack of yams or breadfruit to sell, or other people we know from Port-au-Prince who just come by to talk or listen to politics on the radio with my tonton.

People come and go easily, lightly. I can't get used to any of them. Some of them are good for jokes or rumors. Here's one that Ti Blan, who used to do cash-for-work with Élie before the aid organizations ended cash-for-work, told us last weekend. He'd stopped by and scrubbed his sneakers, and I had given him boiled yam sliced up with herring sauce and a chunk of avocado while he waited for his shoes to dry.

"There's this woman who sends her daughter to school one morning. Then the goudougoudou happens, and the school collapses! The mother runs into the street, crying, 'Anmwèy!' and trying to find her daughter. Then her daughter appears and says, 'Manman, Manman, stop crying! I'm alive! I wasn't at school. I was at my boyfriend's house instead!' And her mother goes, 'Oh, thank God in heaven you're a whore!' "

It's not a very good joke, but we laugh, anyway.

Nadou hardly ever calls, but I know phone cards must be expensive. I can't be angry or impatient. She'll send for me soon. Sometimes I think about all the things Nadine and I will do once she brings me to Miami. I'm making a list, based on the one Nadou and I started as a joke, before.

1. Go to a movie in a theater
2. Go bowling
3. Learn English together
4. Shop at a mall
5. Go to New York City (Brooklyn and Statue of Liberty, too)
6. Ride a roller coaster
7. See snow
8. Meet Rihanna
9. Buy matching purple Converse and high heels
10. Sit in parks (clean parks, no tents) eating ~~ice cream~~ cotton candy
11. Learn to drive a car
12. Go to school!
13. ???

I also keep track of the ways that Port-au-Prince is changing—everything I will tell Nadou when we can talk forever, on and on, face-to-face. The worst is the cholera.

Everyone's terrified of it and telling jokes about it because they're terrified. There is cholera in the provinces, cholera in Cité Soleil, cholera in the camps. Soon we will all have cholera, shitting and shitting and dying, dried-up, in the streets. Where did this cholera come from? Haiti never had cholera before. Why do these things keep happening? Tonton Élie says it's obvious that the foreigners are putting something in our water to make us sick and kill us.

• · • · • · • · •

When I'm not cleaning or sleeping, I read whatever I can find—old schoolbooks or pamphlets left by Jehovah's Witnesses. On the cover they've got smiling people of all different races and colors in a garden with tigers and elephants. Sometimes I nap all afternoon, to make the time pass. There's no point in trying to find the money to go back to school, because Nadine will send for me soon, and I'll have to drop out and move to Miami. I'm waiting until I get to America before I go back to school. Sometimes I wonder if Manman would approve, but she never could have imagined a world in which Nadou and I would be parted.

I simply have to be patient. Whenever my phone vibrates, I hold my breath, hoping that it's Nadou, but it is always Digicel with some offer, or the Ministry of Public Health with an announcement, or a robot message from some presidential candidate. It's always stupid. It's never a person, because there is no one left who remembers me.

Today when I went to hang the laundry out to dry, I passed by Ti Zwit, the old, old man who sits under the eucalyptus tree all day. His eyes are so old they're a cloudy almost-blue. He is so old he's even outlived his own children; he has no family left, so everyone else takes care of him however they can. His knees are as dusty and knotted as the old wooden walking stick that leans against them. "Bonswa, Ti Zwit!" I have to shout, because he can hardly hear. "*How are you doing!*"

"Oh, not too bad, my child!" he smiles, toothlessly.

"*It's Magdalie!*"

"Yes, yes!"

I'm pretty sure he has no idea who I am.

"*Are you eating, Ti Zwit?*"

"Oh, yes, oh yes, my child. I eat."

I reach for his hand and press two fifty-centime pieces into his dry, hard palm. It's barely anything, but it's all I've got.

"God bless you, pitit!" says Ti Zwit. "May God protect you always!"

When I get home, I call Nadine. I have been saving up money, a few gourdes here and there. If I go out to buy Kotex, Tonton Élie doesn't have any idea how much it costs, so I can keep ten gourdes that way. Finally, today, I have enough to put minutes on my phone to call Nadine.

"Sista!" I cry when she finally picks up.

"Chouchou," she says. Her voice sounds like it does when she has a secret.

"Sister, how are you? I've been longing to hear from you."

"I'm good, wi." She doesn't sound excited to hear from me. "How is everybody there?"

"We're the same. Everyone's the same," I tell her, because how can I explain how it really feels? "Have you become totally American yet, boubou?"

Nadine giggles. "I don't even speak English yet."

"Are you taking classes?"

"Of course," Nadine replies. "At what they call community college. They always have the air conditioner on inside, so I have to wear a sweater, and I still feel like I'm getting a cold. But there're so many people in the class who speak Spanish. Hondurans, Dominicans, Cubans . . . I think I should learn Spanish before I learn English. All I've learned so far is *coño*."

"What's that?"

"I think it's a bad word."

"That's funny, Nadou."

"And they look at me funny because I'm Haitian. Like they think I'm dirty."

"Oh, that can't be true, Nadou. You're imagining it."

"Oh? We had to have a conversation in English to introduce ourselves, and when I said, 'I call myself Nadine, and I come from the country of Haiti,' this guy from Colombia said, 'That's a very bad place.'"

"You just didn't know enough English to understand him."

"Mmm . . ." I can hear Nadine shaking her head, all the way in Miami. "They think we're savages with AIDS who don't eat anything but dirt."

I laugh. "Listen, are you getting my visa soon? So I can come join you in your freezing classroom and learn Spanish, too?"

"Soon, soon!" Nadine promises. "I just need to figure things out first. I don't know how to take the bus downtown yet. There's a lot I have to learn before I can do it right—you understand?"

"Yeah, I understand."

"Okay, cheri? Just be patient. Be a little patient."

"Wi, Nadou." Yes, I will be patient.

THE OTHER DAY TONTON ÉLIE SAID, "I THINK maybe I'll send for Michlove so she can help you here."

I said, "Ah. Hmm."

Michlove is his girlfriend from the country, from near Jérémie, where he and Manman grew up. She is about eighteen, but she looks like a big attractive woman, huge tits and a real bounda, a bottom you could balance a basket on. She's not very smart. I know I'm a lot smarter. It's not only that she can't read and write; there are a lot of people who are intelligent who never had a chance to learn to read. Manman was one of them. No, Michlove is just kind of . . . boring. You look into her eyes, and there's no spirit there. So I know I'm supposed to be nice and patient with her. But I know if she comes to Port-au-Prince, I'm going to fight with her all the live-long day about stupid little things, and she's a lot bigger than me and fights with her nails.

So I told Élie, "Ah. Hmm," in a way that showed him that I was resigned to whatever he decided to do. And then, to be fair, I added, "Michlove is very good at braiding hair."

I don't want new friends. I don't want anyone. Not now, anyway. I used to be friendly, but now I am not. Everyone is annoying. Everyone else in the camp is always in and out of one anothers' tents, borrowing things, gossiping, telling jokes, watching soccer games or *Kirikou* reruns on TV, bringing one another food. There are people who, if you don't stop by and say hi for two days, admonish you with, "Oh, I never see you!" or, "You've let me go, have you?" I just want to be by myself, hiding, until Nadou sends me word that I can come join her in America. So that's what I do: I stay inside, sleeping, and waiting for the days to go by.

JANUARY 2011

BAM-BAM-BAM-BAM-BAM!

I sit up straight, my heart pounding, wrenched from sleep. It's two P.M., but it gets so stiflingly hot and dusty under plastic tarps and sheet metal that I'm lying on a sheet on the floor, wearing just a bra and a skirt, sweating, dreaming quick, shallow, afternoon dreams. I am the only one home.

BAM-BAM-BAM-BAM!

It takes me a dazed moment to realize that the noise is someone pounding on the door. I get chills, despite the heat.

"Who is it?" I call out, and I hear the panic in my own voice.

"PNH! Open up now!"

The police? I haven't done anything. Why are the police here? I don't think I've done anything wrong. I reach for the nearest shirt and pull it on, inside out. What if they rape me? What if they shoot me?

"Open up!"

"Wi, wi, map vini! Yes, yes, I'm coming!"

Barefoot, my hair a mess, I stagger to the door and unlock it, and it flies open. There are three officers holding rifles and wearing camouflage and silver reflective sunglasses. Beyond their uniforms and guns, I can't see anything else. If you were to ask me later whether they were short or tall or young or old or black or brown, I wouldn't be able to tell you.

"Bonswa," I say, "Good afternoon," because I'm not sure what else to do.

They don't say anything. They move past me. I am sure they can hear my heart beating. They start searching everywhere. They open the suitcases where we store our clothes and dig into everything. They look under the table and peer into our water buckets and even run their hands over our sacks of rice and charcoal. They pull the mattress off the bed and search beneath it. They poke the butts of their guns against the tarp and metal roof, making sure there's nothing up there. "Mèsi, madmwazèl," one of them says. "Thank you, miss." Then they leave. A few moments later, I hear the same pounding at Mme Joseph's next door. They probably weren't here for more than two minutes, but I feel exhausted, with my eyes wide open. The room is humid, a soupy mix of sweat and men's cologne.

Later I go out to buy hot pepper, green onion, and a

piece of coconut to cook dinner before Tonton Élie gets home. Mme Christophe, the machann with graying hair and green eyes she says she inherited from a French great-grandfather, is gossiping with Michael, the young guy in a red Digicel vest who sells scratchable phone cards. They sound more interested than traumatized.

"Mezanmiiii, I thought I was going to have a heart attack," says Mme Christophe with satisfaction.

"They're looking for thieves and kidnappers," reports Michael. "You heard about the girl who got kidnapped on her way home from school last week near Kalfou Gerald? They're looking for whoever took her."

"Oh, why would anyone kidnap a little innocent?" Mme Christophe mutters, more to herself than anyone else. "What money can her family have?"

"The police were looking for guns, for anyone with guns," Michael says.

"Look at this country," Mme Christophe tsks, shaking her head.

I don't feel like gossiping or talking politics right now, so I buy what I need and thank Mme Christophe and tell them both good afternoon.

When I get home, I notice it, lying on the floor, halfway under the bed. Open, dusty, ruffled, and still, like a dead bird half-eaten by a cat. It's my old journal, the one I've been hiding since it was pulled from the rubble. The police must have shaken it loose when they pulled the mattress from the bed frame.

I stare at it for a while, not sure what to do. The cover,

with yellow puppies on it, is gouged and dusty, but the notebook is intact. I step closer. It's open to a page with one of Nadine's drawings.

I can't help laughing. Since the earthquake, the journal had become a holy, untouchable thing to me, like a relic, but when I see Nadine's stupid drawing of Mme Faustin, it comes back to life. Little grains of whitish plaster fall onto my skirt as I lay the notebook on my lap and begin, cautiously, to leaf through it. And there we are—Manman, Nadine, and me, frozen in time. I run my fingers over the words, the barely-there indentations of the ballpoint pen, and wonder at the things that survive.

Memories are ambushing me. It's been one year this month.

If I'm going to be honest, I'd say I'm afraid of the notebook. Now I'm crying. I can't stop crying; my nose is running, and hot tears are splashing down onto the paper, making the ink bleed.

I miss you. I miss you all over again.

Our souls rise from the pages like smoke. My heart hurts. I know that I am the only one left. The house where it all took place is gone. But for one afternoon, at least, we are together again—my mother, my sister, and me.

DECEMBER 2009

WHEN MME FAUSTIN'S ROOSTER STARTED kek-kek-kede-ing in the middle of the night, I groped around in the dark for my phone to check the time and accidentally elbowed Nadine in the face.

"Se pa fòt mwen," I whispered, even though it was my fault. But what I really meant was "I didn't do it on purpose." Without really waking, Nadine rolled over, flipped her pillow to the cool side, and burrowed down like a little chicken in a dust bath.

Now I am awake, thanks to the rooster, so I am writing by the light of my phone. It's three in the morning on a Monday, and I want to go back to sleep, to get in two more hours before we have to get up and get ready for school, but my eyes are wide open. Nadine's fingernails are still painted—alternating nails, blue, green, and yellow, the colors of the Brazilian flag. We're both fans of the Brazilian soccer team. She'd better not forget to take off the polish before going to school, or they'll suspend her and send her home for the day.

Manman was yelling at her yesterday, telling her to take off the nail polish, but Nadou said, "I can't. I'm all out of acetone," and Manman said, "Well, didn't Élie leave a bottle of paint thinner around here someplace, child?" So Nadou will have to use that, instead.

My scalp feels tight and itchy from the ti kouri Nadine did for me yesterday. I hear Manman starting to move around, on the next bed. She's swatting mosquitoes in the dark as they touch down on her skin, and that's how I know she's awake.

I can hear Manman's knees crack as she sits up in bed and stretches. She unties the kerchief she wraps around her hair at night to keep her hair from frizzing. As she slips out of the bedroom, she picks up the plastic kivèt we pee in at night and goes to empty it in the garden, under the banana tree. It's still dark out; the stars must still be shining brightly.

Manman has to get up early to start the charcoal fire; it takes a long time to heat up. It's too cold for her to bathe, but as the charcoal heats up, she'll splash water on her face and under her arms and between her legs. (Ever since we were little tiny things, Manman has told us that no matter how little water you have, you have to wash your chouchoun twice a day. Any woman who doesn't wash herself down there twice a day is a nasty salòp.) Then she'll start cooking. Probably eggs fried with onions and spices for Mme Faustin (with bread and coffee and sliced avocado and fresh orange juice), and then spaghetti with sliced hot dog and sweet coffee for me and Nadine. Manman says she eats after we leave, but I almost never see her eating. She drinks coffee with lots and lots of sugar. She says it keeps her full all day. Okay, I'm going to stop now and go cut onions for Manman and get dressed. There's no way I'm getting back to sleep.

• · • · • · • · •

School was fine today. As Nadou and I walked up to the road, we stopped as usual to buy pink Tampicos and packets of crackers. The crazy man across the street who is there every morning likes to make loud kissing sounds at all the schoolgirls: "Mmm, mmm, cheri, I've got some cake! I'll give you a little bit of cake if you suck me off!" It is disgusting that he says this to us, and even more disgusting when he does it to the primary-school girls who aren't even young women yet.

"Oh, shut your jaw, and go home, you crazy old bastard!" shouted the lady selling the drinks and snacks, standing up with her hands on her hips. She turned to us as we counted out our gourdes. "Don't pay any attention to him, cheri'm yo. His head isn't right."

"I know," Nadine told her. "We're used to him."

As we walked on, I got this urge to sing. It was such a beautiful day. The sky looked so clear and blue, and the air smelled new. I started to sing a silly children's song about breadfruit and okra sauce, which is what everyone eats in Jérémie, the place we come from in the countryside.

Lam polo, veritab polo,
Sòs kalalou a pare
Moun Jeremi yo sove!
Woy!

"It seems that moun Jeremi are the only people who are saved, eh, Magda?" teased Nadine.

We had dictées today in class. Dictation is boring.

1. L'île d'Haïti a été découverte dans l'année mille quatre-cents quatre-vingt douze par Christophe Colon, un explorateur italien.

2. Ma mère a trois poulets rouges et une vache noire.
3. ‹‹Les mangues sont extraordinaires!›› Colette exclama.

I get distracted and wonder about the people in the dictées. I would like to know what the mother is going to do with her three red hens and her single black cow. Are the hens laying eggs? Does the cow give milk? Is she going to make a living now? Now that she's got the hens and the cow, will she be able to make enough money to send her children to school and buy medicine for them if they get sick? Why is Colette so excited about these particular mangoes?

Sometimes I wonder too much about the people in the dictées and I miss the next one, or I miss something Soeur Altagrace has said. But it's not a very big problem for me, because I am good at French, and good at Creole, too. Not like Nadou, who mixes up her orthography all the time, writing Creole with French spellings.

It's nighttime now. Moths flutter stupidly in the light of the kerosene lamp, stalked by the fat, translucent geckos on the wall. I try to concentrate on my history homework but can't. I'm supposed to be writing an essay about the French colonizers who enslaved our ancestors and how the slaves had a revolution to liberate themselves, and then Jean-Jacques Dessalines said that now we were the masters of this land. But all I can hear is Mme Faustin and her guests, upstairs in the main part of the house. I've put on my headphones and turned up the volume on the MP3 player Nadine bought on the street with money her papa sent her. I don't understand the English words, but I sing along, anyway. I love Beyoncé. (Note: I will have a baby someday and ask Beyoncé to be the godmother.)

Nadine has laid out her school uniform on the bed and is wait-

ing for the electricity to come on so she can iron. She irons her uniform every night, concentrating on each pleat in the skirt.

Even with the music in my ears, the voices upstairs are distracting and I can't concentrate, even though I love history and writing. I am no good at math, though. It has too many numbers, and they confuse me. Nadou is better at it than I. Sometimes I think that if some doctor could just combine my brain and Nadine's, we'd be a genius girl—sometimes I think that maybe when we were in the womb, Nadine got all of one kind of intelligence and I got all of another kind of intelligence, and then I remember that we were never in the womb together in the first place.

The loud voices belong to some out-of-town visitors who have come to visit Mme Faustin. Manman is in the upstairs kitchen. Hearing the clatter of china and silverware, I picture Manman, hair hastily braided and sticking out in ten different directions, wearing a mismatched pèpè blouse and skirt, pouring soup into bowls and placing them on a tray, filling a jug with treated ice water. Manman's back is bothering her again, and Nadine or I will rub it with Vicks and maskrèti oil later tonight. She claims the combination of menthol and castor oil helps relieve the soreness.

On ordinary days, if Mme Faustin goes to bed early, Manman lets me and Nadou slip upstairs and watch a soap opera in the empty living room, as long as we keep the volume low and sit on the floor, not the furniture. Then Manman comes and joins us on the floor, barefoot in her thin white cotton nightdress. The one we've been watching lately is about Margarita, who works as a maid in a handsome doctor's brother's fiancée's mother's house (I think), and the woman is a demon, a nasty demon, even worse than Mme Faustin, our own demon here in this house. That's my favorite part of the soaps. No matter how unjust, scheming, and hateful the villains, you know they're going to get it in the end.

No TV tonight, though. The visitors are talking late with Mme Faustin. No one has explained to us who these people are. They are simply more people to serve.

"Haiti is filthy now," Mme Faustin is saying. Her voice echoes from the dining room, bouncing like a rubber ball out the window and caroming down into our basement room. "Everything used to be clean. Haitians were classy and respectful when Duvalier was still in control. Even though we were poor, we had dignity! The poor used to be happy. They didn't think to ask why they didn't have much. They didn't know they were poor. They were happy and clean. Now they're all criminals."

I can't say if it is true that the streets used to be clean. I know I've never seen them clean. There are always soda bottles and Chiritos packages and little plastic bags, discarded after people drink the treated water from them, collecting and growing dusty along curbsides and filling up the sewers—but where else are people supposed to throw them when there are no public trash cans? I can't believe that people never knew they were poor. It's what we are; it's what we call ourselves, even. The poor, the unfortunate.

"I'm lucky I got a good one," Mme Faustin continues. "Yolette is loyal to me. She loves me. She gets me a glass of water before I even say I'm thirsty. Most people can't trust their servants anymore. They're the first ones to turn on you, to steal all your jewelry or shoot you in your bed."

I hear footsteps overhead, Manman's familiar rhythm as she moves from place to place, laying out the plates. We won't eat until the guests have eaten and the dishes are cleared, and we won't sleep until Mme Faustin goes to bed.

I'll go help Manman in the kitchen. I'll finish this later. I just have to make sure that Mme Faustin doesn't see me. She doesn't like to see me or Nadine doing anything around her house. She says, "I won't have any restavèk children working in my house!" Apparently it's okay to make Manman work her fingers to the bone, but if a child under eighteen so much as scrapes a plate, it's a human rights violation.

It's past midnight now, and Manman just came slowly down the stairs a few minutes ago and rinsed herself with cold water from the garden spigot. The radio's on, and we will keep it on after we brush our teeth and climb into bed. Manman's favorite station plays slow love songs—in French, in Spanish, in English; it doesn't matter, as long as it's sentimental and sweet, sweet-sweet-sweet like dous makòs. I am lucky. We're poor, but there are people who are poorer. I know that I am blessed.

These words are in my handwriting. They were written by my hand, but they were not written by the same girl I am today. That Magdalie, she had a normal life, she had homework, she had a mother and a sister. That Magdalie didn't know that her school would collapse, floor upon floor upon floor, like a house of cards. I don't recognize her. I don't recognize myself. And I hate this; I hate it all. I want my life back. I want to worry about ordinary things like algebra and French dictées again. I want everyone back and whole and alive.

But sooner or later I am pulled back into waking reality. *I'm here, without you.* The white flecks that came off the journal stick to my skin like ash.

FEBRUARY 2011

ORDINARY LIFE NOW IS LIKE A BAD PARODY of ordinary life before the earthquake—a worse, distorted version of the way things used to be. The other day, Tonton Élie said, "Why don't we go to Kanaval?" and I said, "Why bother?" There are still floats throwing T-shirts to the crowds, there are still bands, there are still people covered in glitter and sequins, dancing all night through the streets—but now the parades wind through the camp on the Champ de Mars where thousands of people live under tarps. The city government put up barriers all around the camp to make it harder to see from the parade, but everyone knows it's there. Why do they try to trick us into being joyful? Nothing is the way it's supposed to be.

Last night, as Tonton Élie was fixing the wiring in an old TV set while listening to commentators talk politics on Radio Kiskeya, I said to him, "Tonton, I don't know if it will be possible, but I want to be in school again." My heart was pounding.

Tonton Élie didn't look up.

"Tonton?"

"Michlove is getting bigger," he said.

"Okay . . ."

"After she has the baby, I'm going to bring her here. She says she's always worrying about me here. If she keeps worrying, it'll make her milk spoil."

"And so?"

He put down his screwdriver. "And so. I'll see what I can do, Magdalie."

Tonton Élie tries to be nice to me, but both of us know that we wouldn't be living together if we hadn't been forced to. He does quiet, kind things: he leaves me the bigger plantain, even though he works all day, and he lets me have the mattress, even though Nadou is gone. But he can't do much for me. He can't be Manman. He can't be Nadine. He can't give me my old life back, and that is what I really want.

He doesn't even realize it is my birthday today.

What he said to me this morning as he left to see about a job was, "Are you washing laundry today, Magdalie?" He's always going to see about a job, because cash-for-work is over now, and he can fix only so many old radios. "Use bleach to get my shoelaces white. I can't go leaving my CV places if I look like a peasant."

"We don't have any bleach, Tonton."

"So get some bleach!"

"Give me money to get a bag of bleach if you want bleach!"

"Degaje w, pitit! Figure it out, Magdalie! Do I have to do everything around here? Every burden of this family is on my back?"

"I'm not your servant! Don't treat me like some dog, some restavèk in this house!" I screamed.

My anger made him angrier. "If you're lucky, I'll send you to be a maid in someone else's house, and they'll feed you leftovers, and you'll sleep on the floor. Is that what you want?"

"What I want? What I *want*, Tonton? When has it ever mattered what I want?"

Tonton Élie ran his hands over his short hair, as if he was trying to rub away his frustration; he ran his fingers over his chin stubble, which is just beginning to show tiny dots of white. "Magdalie, I know this isn't fair. But it's not just you. You understand? Life is hard for everyone."

He was right, but I didn't want to be reasonable. "Now you're saying I'm selfish? You don't know what's inside me. You don't know. You know, they say that only the knife knows what's in the core of a yam. You don't know what's in my heart!"

"Eh, bien, you never tell me a damn thing!"

"Why should I?"

"I should send you away," Tonton Élie grumbled. "One less thing for me to worry about." He slammed the door, and our neighbors all pretended not to hear.

That's how it is in the camp—you pretend you're not inches away from your neighbors and separated by a thin sliver of wood or a tarp as thin as a sheet. You hear every laugh, every fart, every moan, every fight, and every breath, but you act as if you don't hear it, and they do the same for you.

Or sometimes they don't. People are nosy. Jilène who does pedicures said, "Oh-oh, Magdalie, are you fighting with your uncle again?"

I said, "It's not your business." Oh, I've become so mouthy, so nasty these days.

Jilène shook her head and said, "There are children on the street because they don't have anybody. Anybody at all. Thank Jesus you don't have to sell your body on the street, child. Thank Jesus you're not dying of hunger."

That is how I am celebrating my birthday: a fight with Tonton Élie and a lecture from Jilène. When Manman was alive, even though she never had money for cake, she would boil sweet potatoes in milk with sugar and cinnamon for our birthdays. Now there's none of that. All I want is for Nadine to call. She is the only one who matters.

The thing I really want to tell Nadine, if she remembers my birthday, is "The water buckets are so much heavier since you left," but I don't know if that would make sense to her, and I don't know why that's the thing I want to say. "The buckets are heavier. The roads are longer. The dust is dustier. The burned rice is harder to scrub off the bottom of the pot. Everything has changed since you left."

Today in front of me in the water line is a pregnant girl around my age. I've never seen her before. She's got cinnamon skin and a too-prominent breastbone that makes me think of a tiny bird. She looks as if any little thing could crush her. Her belly is huge, so huge on her skin and bones.

"Bonjou," she says.

"Bonjou," I reply in greeting.

"Mezanmi, the sun is hot!"

"The sun is always hot," I reply, because it's the expected reply.

The skinny pregnant girl smiles at me, friendly and eager. "I'm Safira. Louis Safira."

"I'm Magdalie."

"I just came here," she explains. "I'm staying with my auntie."

"Okay," I reply.

She keeps on smiling at me, even though I don't want to talk. "Who do you live with?"

"My uncle."

"It's not the best, no? My auntie is nice enough, but I'm not really used to her. If I could still stay with my mama, I would," Safira chatters. "But it's not possible. Like they say, 'When you've got no mother, you nurse from your grandma!'" She giggles.

"Mmm," I reply. She must be bored or lonely to be talking to someone with a face like mine, I think, because I know I look angry.

"She doesn't mistreat me or anything, though. She doesn't beat me or order me around. And she cooks really well. Even if all she's got is a chicken neck and a couple of half-rotten sweet plantains, she can make enough for five people! She's good!"

"That's nice."

"You know they always say, 'Bay piti pa chich.' Giving just a little isn't being stingy. We're all doing what we can."

"You speak in proverbs, like an old woman."

Safira laughs. "There is wisdom in the mouths of the old."

"You're still doing it!" I start laughing, too. "Today's my birthday," I say suddenly. "I'm seventeen today."

"Really?" Safira's eyes widen. "Bonne fête!" She says this French "Happy Birthday" ridiculously. Then she starts singing, loudly: "Bon anniversaire, nos vœux les plus sinceres!"

"Stop it, stop it! Don't do that, please!"

"Why not?"

"It's embarrassing!"

She grins, a wide, trusting smile, with the skin stretched over all the bones in her face. "It's your birthday! Are you having a party?"

"No."

"Are you having cake?"

"No. Who's going to buy me a cake?"

"So at least you need someone to sing for you."

"It doesn't matter."

"Of course it matters! Another year on earth!"

Her words echo through all the emptiness inside me. I feel so sad, I can hardly speak.

"When will you come to my house?" Safira asks.

"What?"

"You should come to my house. It's an ugly little house, but you're my friend, aren't you?"

"I don't go out very much . . . ," I mumble.

Safira looks at me in a funny way. I think her expression might hold pity, but I don't know why she should pity me. "Well, you know, you're welcome, whenever. You're my friend."

"Okay."

Finally Safira finishes filling her water bucket and balances it on her head with one hand. "Bye-bye, Magdalie! And happy birthday, cheri!"

"Bye."

What is *her* story? I begin to imagine. Some nice-looking guy on the street with a sweet smile called her doudou, and she thought the endearment meant he loved her. He promised her affection, he promised he'd take care of her, and he promised she'd never be hungry again. It *felt* like love. But when she got pregnant, he turned his back on her and disappeared. It happens all the time. Manman knew that. That's why she warned me and Nadou all the time.

I've got five gourdes in my pocket, and on the way home I buy a little bag of fried sweet potato from stout Grimèl, who sells good fritay off a wide metal tray on the corner. Everyone calls her Grimèl because that's her color, like coffee with a little Carnation milk stirred into it; I have no idea what her real name is. She has a whole band of children, including a little boy called Bouboul because he's so round; I have no idea what his real name is, either.

"How are you, cheri?" Grimèl asks me. "How are all your people?"

"Everyone's fine, wi," I tell her, because sometimes it's easier to give short answers. "And your people?"

"Oh, you know. Saïka had a cold, but she's better now, thanks to God. Besides that, everyone's still here."

I stuff the sweet potato into my mouth quickly before I get home, even though it burns my tongue, because I don't want Élie to know I'm eating food without sharing. It's my birthday present to myself.

By the time I get home, there's a red dent across my palm from the heavy water bucket. I stretch my fingers, open and close my hand. Tonton Élie is back. He is out working behind the tent; I can tell by the fumes of paint thinner wafting in the afternoon heat. They sting my eyes and make the world shimmer.

"Magda, come here so I can talk to you," he calls. His voice has that funny sound in it, the sound of bad news he's trying to cover up.

"Wi, Tonton."

"Look, Magdalie," he says, clearing his throat. "You know Michlove. I have to start thinking about the baby. I've got to bring her to Port-au-Prince after she delivers; I don't want the baby growing up in the provinces."

I nod.

"So that's something we need to discuss. Michlove is my responsibility, right? She's my priority."

I nod again. My chest feels tight, and I'm waiting for the bad news.

"I won't have money for your school, Magdalie. I just won't have the cash."

"Okay," I say.

"There's no work in this country."

"I know."

"You're angry."

"No."

"You're disappointed."

I don't have anything else to say. I can't argue. There is nothing to argue about. I don't have the right to feel any of those things. There is no money. I know there is no money.

I go inside the tent and lie down on the bed, my face in the pillow. The pillow smells like paint thinner. *No school. No school.*

I am alone, I am alone, I am alone. If I fall, there will be no one to catch me. I am responsible for myself. I have to be an adult now. No more birthdays. I can't think about childish things. My old life feels like a film I saw while half asleep. Memories splash through my mind, but they aren't my life anymore: buying new notebooks for school every year and covering them with plastic so they wouldn't get dirty or ripped. Chasing Nadine around Mme Faustin's muddy backyard, through the banana leaves and the mango trees, threatening to poke her with my new pencil. Washing my school uniform every afternoon, laying my socks out flat in the sun so they'd be dry before the next morning. *I am alone.* It is only now, in Manman's absence, that the sacrifices she made, every single day, have become visible to me. And every time another layer of her quiet sacrifice is peeled away, I miss her all over again. The loss makes me feel at once so heavy and so empty.

It is late now. My birthday is over, and Nadine never called.

I WROTE A LETTER TO MANMAN TODAY. SHE never knew how to read and write when she was alive, but I don't think that matters anymore. I think that Manman will understand everything now—there's no such thing as illiteracy after you die, only understanding. I think the words will go to her—not even the words themselves, but what the words mean. But I wrote it in Creole, anyway, not in French, because if I were talking to her, I would have done it in Creole. I worry that I'm forgetting her. I can still see her face, but it's getting harder to remember her voice. Sometimes I panic, because she is nowhere, because I don't know where she is, because she doesn't exist in the world. But sometimes Manman is everywhere. Manman is in the sharp *thwack, thwack, thwack* of the wooden mortar pounding spices, and in the softer, stickier, deeper *thwack, thwack, thwack*

of breadfruit wedges getting beaten into doughy yellow tonmtonm. She is in the drumbeats that echo through the twisting, slippery corridors of the bidonvilles and in the blare of horns in the rara parades drifting unseen from downtown during Kanaval. She is in the smell of vanilla essence and in the sound of the rain ricocheting off the tarp and sheet metal at dusk.

Manman cheri, I love you so much. I regret that I didn't tell you that every day. I want you to know that I am doing okay. I am sad that you never knew that Nadine and I survived. It hurts me, because I know that your last thoughts must have been of us. Please don't be scared anymore—don't be scared for us. We are getting by. Nadine is in America. She doesn't call very much, but don't worry, I won't let her go. Even if she's far away. She says she'll send for me soon. I'll take care of her now because you didn't get to finish taking care of her. I miss you. Now that you're gone, I know what you meant to me. I want to thank you, because even though you never got to finish raising me, if I am a decent and good person today, if I am educated today, it is because of you. I love you. And I miss you. I LOVE YOU. I'm sad, I'm angry, I'm crying. I'm crying so much, I can't see these words anymore. I love you. Magda

Then I burned the letter. It felt private and sacred; I didn't want anyone to see it. The paper glowed like bright orange lace as the smoke rose toward heaven, and as the paper was transformed into soft wisps of gray, I closed my eyes and imagined the words finding

Manman and uniting with her soul in an unseen place. I pressed my fingertips into the cool ashes and felt them crumble like velvet dust, then wiped my fingers across my forehead and up and down my arms.

I wrote a letter to Nadine, too. Which isn't worth looking at again. It is so filled with shapeless anger that I'm ashamed to think of it. I ripped it up and threw it into one of the portable toilets. But I remember how it ends.

I will come to you. I will come to Miami. Somehow I will. You have forgotten me, Nadou, but I won't forget you.

MARCH 2011

"WE CAN'T STAY IN THIS CAMP," TONTON Élie declares suddenly this morning as he spits his toothpaste into the rivulet of dirty water, as brown and cloudy as stale coffee, running down the sidewalk outside our tent.

"Tonton?" I blow on the charcoal, and it glows red; I'm scrambling an egg for us to share.

He dries his face on a towel. "Have you heard, Magda? Ti Zwit died last night."

"Oh! Poor old man! Like that? Dying without being sick?"

"They say it was cholera." Tonton Élie whistles softly, sucking between his teeth. "This cholera! Where did this germ come from? How can it live in this heat of this camp when everyone else is being grilled alive under the sun?"

"I don't know, Tonton. Did he die in the camp?"

"They took him to the clinic. No one wanted to touch him; they were afraid. He was covered in shit, shit everywhere, soaking him like water. He died by the time they got to the clinic."

"Poor old man . . . ," I murmur again.

After Tonton Élie leaves, I take out my old journal and flip to the end. How could Ti Zwit live so long and then die from some microbe the country of Haiti had never seen before? My tonton is right—we've got to get out of this camp. But I have to go farther. I'm not staying in the camp, or in Port-au-Prince, or in this country. I'm going to Miami as soon as I can.

WAYS TO MAKE MONEY
— sell things (water?)
— clean houses
— rich boyfriend

That last idea, "rich boyfriend," is a joke. There are plenty of girls who do it, some even as young as me. But I never would. Manman would kill me if I did that. She'd say it's really no different from being a whore. Even worse, maybe he wouldn't be rich at all, just some smooth guy who spins sweet words, and I'd end up pregnant and skinny like Safira.

Maybe I could clean someone's house, but I don't want to, not yet. I don't want to be humiliated like that. I don't want to end up like Manman. But everyone is trying to get those jobs, because even a humiliating job is better than starving.

I can't sell anything in the public markets because I don't have the money to rent a spot. Even a tiny, crowded, muddy spot, squatting on a low chair in the sun. And all those ladies have been there forever; they all know one another; they all helped each other get their spots there. I couldn't just show up with a pile of coconuts or a stack of hot peppers and start selling them.

I could sell things on the street. But it has to be something easy, so Tonton Élie won't know about it. I don't have the money to make candies or snacks like boiled breadfruit nuts, and even if I did, Tonton Élie would see that I was doing it. That leaves selling treated water, or maybe little packets of chewing gum. Everybody needs water; nobody *needs* chewing gum. I should sell water. Even though it is so, so heavy . . . But I'll need help getting started.

After I wash all the dishes and scrape the burned remains of last night's rice out of the cooking pot, I sprinkle a little kerosene on the ground to keep the flies away, and I padlock the plywood door to the tent. I've shined my shoes and put on one of Nadou's old blouses—shiny, light purple with black stripes. It's too loose on me, but I don't have time to bring in the seams.

Jimmy's house is visible from the camp, a two-story concrete building that rises out of the cité—*in* the cité but maybe not *part* of it. It only got a few cracks in the earthquake. Some people are luckier than others. The house has its own gate and a water reservoir in the back; it's painted pale pink and white, like a frosted cake. Jimmy's family lives well on the money his papa sends from America.

I rap on the metal gate with a rock I've picked up from the road. After a moment, an eye peeks through the peephole. It's Farah, one of Jimmy's little sisters, who must be around twelve. Her cheeks are round and bright.

"Hi, Magdalie," she says. "Come on in."

"How are you, ti chou?" I ask, kissing her fat cheek.

"Not too bad."

"Is Jimmy here?"

"Yeah, he's studying upstairs. Jim-*my*!"

The lakou looks the way poor people's yards do when they suddenly make some money: cluttered. There is Jimmy's regular car, a beige SUV that's a few years old, and two other cars in the process of being repaired. One has no seats, and one has no wheels. There are a couple of goats tethered in a corner and countless chickens. A big generator sits next to the house, but it isn't running. Scattered toys—a bright plastic tricycle, a baby doll with blue marker all over its face, and a bunch of stuffed animals—fill the floor of the entryway. The back of the house is still unpainted, and there's a big pile of gravel with a shovel stuck in it on the ground. Tonton Élie says that people do such things all the time so they can claim their houses are "unfinished" and they don't have to pay any taxes to the state. I don't know if that's true or not. Maybe they just don't have the money to finish yet.

I sit on the plastic chair in front of the flat-screen TV and wait for Jimmy to come down. There's a stack of bootleg DVDs on the shiny tiled floor—Haitian comedies with Tonton Bicha and Bòs Djo, and American action movies with Steven Seagal and Arnold Schwarzenegger, and some porn.

Jimmy bounces down the stairs, two at a time. "Hey, Magda!" he announces, beaming. He's clutching a psychology textbook in his hand and pulling headphones out of his ears. As he leans in to kiss me on the cheek, I catch a strong whiff of cologne. "How are you? How is everyone?"

"Oh, you know." I smile vaguely. "Fighting against this hard life. And you?"

"Comme si, comme ça. Do you hear from Nadine?"

"Sometimes," I say. I don't want to tell him more than that. I don't even want to admit it to myself, to form the words, to say: *I do not know if Nadou is who I thought she was.* "I think she's doing well."

"Can I get you something to drink?"

"A little water, please."

"You don't want a Couronne? A Sprite?"

"Okay—Sprite."

"Beautiful." Jimmy grins and heads toward the kitchen. He returns with a whole bottle of cold Sprite and a glass.

"So, Magda, how have you been? What are you doing with yourself?"

I cough. Fear lodges in my throat like a lump of poorly pounded tonmtonm. Then the words spill out in a torrent. "Well, Jimmy . . . I'm not really doing anything. Uh . . . I guess that's why I've come here today. My tonton makes a little money sometimes, but it's nothing stable. It's not stable—you understand?" I take a sip of my Sprite, but the cold bubbles make me cough. "He says he can't pay for school for me. And I need to go meet Nadou in Miami, and I don't have the money for the ticket yet. And the way things are going, I'm never going to get the money."

Jimmy nods, his brow furrowed in concern. He leans toward me. I take a deep breath.

"So I need some kind of activity to . . . to make money. You understand? But . . . but I don't even have the money to start."

Jimmy nods again and cracks his knuckles. His hands are big and smooth.

"What kind of activity were you thinking of, Magdalie?"

"I could sell bags of treated water?" This comes out as a question instead of a statement. "It wouldn't be that expensive to start. And I need something that my tonton wouldn't know about. I just . . . I don't want him to know if I've got my own money."

"Do you have a cooler?"

"Not yet, no."

"Okay. We've got an old Igloo out back. I could lend it to you. You'll have to wash it out well with bleach, though."

"Oh, that's fine! That's perfect!"

"And this." Jimmy reaches into the pocket of his loose

blue jeans and pulls out his wallet. He opens it and hands me three 250-gourde bills. "You're going to need to buy the water in bulk."

I feel as if someone has opened a door and flooded my life with light. The money is crisp and clean-smelling. I rub it between my fingers. "This is so kind of you, Jimmy. Thank you, infinitely."

"This isn't a gift, Magda," he warns. "You'll pay me back when you can. But it shouldn't take that long."

"Of course, of course. Still, thank you infinitely! You won't be sorry."

THE NEXT DAY I WAIT FOR TONTON ÉLIE TO leave, but before I can leave myself, Safira, the skinny pregnant girl with cinnamon skin from the water line, appears at our door.

"Bonswa, Magdalie! Do you remember me? I made some mayi moulen with sòs pwa," she says. She is friendly, talkative as a mockingbird. "You want to eat?"

I want to leave, but I can't be rude.

She is so skinny that I feel guilty taking anything from her, but I don't want to embarrass her, so I take the small covered bowl. "Thanks. You can come in."

"I thought maybe you wouldn't remember me," Safira says brightly.

"I remember you," I say. She doesn't know how few people I speak to these days; my voice has rusted. Her desperate enthusiasm frightens me, that she wants so much to be friends.

"Who did you say you live with?" Safira asks.

"My tonton," I say.

"Just your uncle?"

"Yes." I don't say anything more than that.

"My manman sent me here to stay with my auntie when she figured out I was pregnant," she says. "She thought I'd get aid if I was in the camp. So I stay with my auntie and her two little boys. We're on the other side, near the entrance. I watch the boys for her. They're naughty! But they go to preschool during the day."

"Where were you before?"

"Belekou, in Cité Soleil."

Cité Soleil, the sprawling shantytown down by the sea in Port-au-Prince. Mme Faustin used to say the gangsters boiled people alive and ate them there, but Manman said it wasn't true, that the people there were simply very poor, just like us, or even poorer. "Where's your auntie right now?" I ask.

"She goes to buy vegetables during the week in Cabaret, to sell at the market downtown. So I take care of the little boys and bathe them and walk them to school."

"So you're alone most of the time?"

She smiles. "I always have God."

I don't know what else to say. "Let me beep you," I finally say. "Then you'll have my number in your phone."

Safira grins, revealing her chipped front tooth. "Okay! Where do you go to the market?"

"Sometimes in Delmas 32, sometimes downtown."

"If you want to walk to 32 together sometime . . ."

"Sure."

"That's good! I get so bored walking alone, you know."

I don't want to be bound to her, but I find myself confessing my secret, as though, if I don't speak these words aloud to someone, I won't know if anything is real.

"Safira?"

"Yeah?"

"I'm going to Miami. I'm going to go live with my sister in Miami."

"Oh, Magdalie! When?"

"Not quite yet. My sister is going to get me a visa, and then I'm going to buy a ticket."

Safira's eyebrows jump. "You have money?"

"Not yet. I mean, that's what I'm working on right now. I'm going to do a little commerce. My cousin's friend Jimmy gave me a little help. I'm going to sell water."

"Around here?"

"No! No, and don't say anything. I don't want my uncle to find out. Please don't tell anybody. I'll go downtown."

Safira stops smiling.

"What about it?"

She shakes her head slowly. "You know it's not safe."

"Ah, nothing is safe. Let me tell you, my friend. You can be hiding in your house, minding your own business, and the roof can collapse and crush you flat. We don't control any of it."

"That doesn't mean you have to *look* for problems, Magdalie."

I smile. "I'll be fine. And I'm not doing it forever. Just until I get enough money for the plane ticket."

Safira looks as if she has something more to say, but she stops herself, then says quietly, "Okay. Well, say hi to all your people from me!" And she leaves, lightly, despite the swell of her belly. Her narrow back curves inward with the weight.

I twist an old T-shirt into a flat, round roll and balance it on the top of my head. Then I set the old red Igloo cooler on top of it. When I steady it with one hand, it doesn't feel as heavy as I had expected. The Igloo is filled with a hundred little plastic bags of Alaska drinking water, packed with ice and salt and wrapped in burlap to keep them cold.

"Bwe dlo, bwe dlo, bwe dlo!" I call. *"Drink water, drink water, drink water!"* I force my voice to the front of my mouth. It comes out nasal, but it carries far. Still, I sound like a child. I never sound like a child in my own head, but when I hear my voice amid the cacophony of downtown Port-au-Prince's streets and all the other merchants and noises there, it is high and startled, like a little girl's.

I work around the Grand-Rue, careful to stay far from the blocks where people I know might be working or shopping. The crowds are so thick here that no one notices me. I haven't sold a single bag of water. Everyone's too busy looking out for themselves—keeping an eye out for thieves, watching for taptaps and old American school buses barreling down the road or turning around on streets that are too narrow for them, pushing their way onto the sidewalks and crushing the machanns' wares. People don't dawdle here. They move as quickly as they can, making sure not to trip over discarded chunks of rubble or kick a skinny street dog or slosh through a rotten pile of garbage. Mango peels, orange peels, Styrofoam oozing milky gray. It is exhausting to pay attention to so many things—to watch your feet and the people around you at the same time. Who would pay attention to another girl selling water?

In my history book, in school—school!—I saw photos of the Grand-Rue as it once was. The photos were black-and-white. The Grand-Rue was a beautiful and civilized place—stately arched doorways and brick facades, wooden balconies overlooking the uncrowded street. The men wore suits and hats, the women wore dresses, and everyone looked clean and unafraid. A ghost image. I try to reconcile it with the commotion around me—the jostling, the garbage, the noise and dust. So many of those buildings have crumbled, burying forever beneath them the Digicel guys selling phone cards, the machann selling plastic sandals or bottles of molasses or hair extensions, the children walking home from school. Vines spring up from the dust—even squash vines and other things you can eat—and wrap themselves around the ruins, in the middle of the city, as though the island were trying to reclaim itself.

I adjust my Igloo on top of my head and continue my promenade. *"Bwe dlo, bwe dlo, bwe dlooo!"* I call. I cannot be shy anymore. There was a time I would have been too shy to take to the streets calling out, but now I am not. Now I am too grown-up to be timid.

"Dlo, dlo, dlo, dlo, dlo!"

"Dlo!" someone calls, a man in a Boston Celtics jersey. I take my Igloo down and hand him three bags of water. The water is so cold, it makes my fingers ache. The man hands me a ten-gourde note, soft, sweaty, and wrinkled with age.

"I don't have any change, msyè," I apologize.

He glares, dumps the water bags back into my cooler, and snatches his money back, sucking his teeth at me. I am an idiot. I should have had a few coins, enough to make change, enough to get started. I want to cry. I want to call after him, "Please, msyè, we can make change somewhere, anywhere . . ." But there are so many water vendors on the street, he's already moved on and bought it from someone else.

The really fearless kids weave in and out of traffic with their buckets of water bags on their heads or in their arms. They stand at the doors of taptaps and the backs of pickup trucks as the passengers get on, and they sell a lot of water that way. They are bold and deft, confident that they won't get run over. I stand on the sidewalk, my back to a wall that smells of pee, and pray. *Dear God, give me the courage to do what they do.* But I can't. My feet are glued to the sidewalk. I can't will myself to walk like Moses into that traffic.

The sun bears down on me, so hot, it prickles. My stomach is so empty, it's gnawing on itself; my mouth waters, and I don't know whether I feel hungry or nauseated. The Igloo is heavy, and I can feel myself growing shorter as the bones of my neck are pressed together. I put the cooler down at my feet.

A pair of giggling schoolgirls approach, arm in arm, wearing the yellow-black-and-red plaid uniform of Collège Marie-Jeanne. I wonder if they are sisters or just friends.

"Dlo!" calls the shorter one. My arms burn as I lift up my Igloo and hurry toward them. She presses a five-gourde coin into my hand, and they tear the plastic bags open with their front teeth and resume their gossip.

They don't see me. My shins are skinny and gray with dust and dried mud, and the hem of my skirt is ragged. They can't see me. A street child, uneducated, dirty and alone, as invisible as a little ghost. *I was just like you,* I want to tell them. *Someday I will be like you again.*

My mouth is dry, and I'm dizzy. One of the taptaps is playing Barikad from a speaker so big, the sound makes my teeth rattle. I take one of my own bags of water from the cooler and suck half of it down. It is so wonderfully cold that I cough from the chill. The rest I squirt over my hair; it dribbles down my forehead and my back.

A dented SUV creaks down the street, bouncing through a pothole and spraying me with thin mud. As the car slows, I hoist my Igloo and call, *"Dlo!"* I hear the door locks click, as if the driver is double-checking that she is protected and safe.

As one tinted window descends, I panic. I know those eyes, even before the window reveals the sour mouth. I want to run away. I can't bear for her to see me like this, with no dignity left, as low and as worthless as she always believed me to be.

"Magdalie?" says Mme Faustin.

I swallow. "Wi, madanm."

"What are you doing here?" It's the voice she used once when I was a little girl and she caught me staring too long at the china figurines on top of the television. A low, punishing voice that says, *You don't belong here.*

"Would you like to buy some water, madanm?"

"That water? Child, have you never heard of cholera?"

"No, this is good water. Potable water. I drink it, and I never get sick."

"You people never know the first thing about hygiene. What are you doing, Magdalie, selling water like some urchin on the street?"

"I . . . um . . . ," I stammer.

"Yolette was a good, clean woman who did honest work, and look what you're doing, standing in the mud." She looks disgusted, her lips curling as if she has just smelled something rotten.

I want to hammer her fat face with my fists, but I can't even make a sound, let alone move.

A kamyonèt driver starts honking and cursing, and the guy selling batteries smacks the side of Mme Faustin's car three times with his open palm. "Are you buying or not? Get outta the way! Don't block the street! Damn!"

She jumps. The tinted window zips up, and she pulls

away into traffic without another word, before I have the chance to tell her she's wrong about everything.

By four in the afternoon the city is a grayish haze, and I've made seventy-five gourdes. It's not a lot, but it is something. It's only my first day. I have plenty of water left to sell. I take my kerchief out and wipe my forehead, and it comes away black with soot. I feel the weight of the coins and wadded-up bills in the pockets of my skirt and hidden in my bra. The weight of promise.

But Mme Faustin's words stick like a fishbone in my throat. What would Manman think now, if she could see me? This is not what she'd hoped for for me. But she had never hoped to die like she did, either.

Even though dusk is still hours away, I've got to get home before Tonton Élie grows suspicious. As I sit in unmoving traffic, in the taptap that goes down Grand-Rue toward Kalfou Aviyasyon, I calculate my profits: five gourdes for this ride, then ten gourdes for another to take me up Delmas. That leaves me with sixty gourdes. Should I buy some fried breadfruit for five gourdes? I am so hungry that my fingertips feel icy, despite the heat. But if I buy a snack, that's less money in my hands . . . And I still need to pay Jimmy back.

I'm leaning my head against the metal grate at the front of the taptap with my eyes closed when a hand clutches my knee and shakes it roughly. "Hey, little girl! *Ti fi!*" Two young men with sweatshirts wrapped around their faces stand at the entrance to the taptap, their eyes hard and blazing. Two small silver guns glint in their hands.

No one says anything; no one fights, because it's more important to live. All the passengers resign themselves; they know what this means, and they take out their purses and their wallets and remove their earrings. The two young men work quickly, snatching the men's wallets, reaching into the women's purses and taking their money, their cell phones, pulling off any jewelry that looks as if it might be valuable. They reach into people's pockets and into women's bras and into the backs of their panties, where some women hide their money. The thief's hand feels small and young as it digs into my bra and finds my crumpled money. He gives my breast a squeeze. I close my eyes and grit my teeth and do not gasp. Then they step off the back of the taptap, back into the traffic, and I watch as all my profits disappear with them.

No one in the taptap says anything for a moment. Finally one man says, "Tèt chaje. What can you do?" A woman responds, "Look at this country," and tsks. I don't say anything. I realize I'm shaking. "Oh, pòdyab, poor little thing, she's trembling!" says a lady next to me. She has a kind voice with a lisp. She strokes my hair as if I were a frightened child. "You'll be okay," she says. "Don't be scared. It's over now."

But I'm not shaking because I'm scared. I'm shaking because I'm furious.

TONIGHT I LIE ON MY BED, REPLAYING WHAT happened and trying to figure out how I will ever get the money to pay Jimmy back. Tonton Élie brings home some spaghetti and tells me to fry it up, but I just turn over and stare at the wall. I smash a mosquito against my thigh, and my palm comes away smeared with bright red blood.

"Did you hear me, Magdalie? I told you to make dinner. Do I have to do everything around here?" I shut my eyes, as though that could keep out the meanness in Tonton Élie's words. "You just lie around here all day, doing nothing. What a lazy child Yolette raised!"

I think of the hard young eyes of the thieves on the taptap. I recognize their fury, because it is my fury, too. If you get hungry enough, poor enough, desperate enough, you can do anything. Even steal. Even kill.

I flip over and glare at my uncle, as if daring him to challenge me.

"Lazy! Useless!" Tonton Élie spits the words. Then he stops, and a strange look comes over his face. He is suddenly old and tired. He drops the package of dry spaghetti on the bed and stalks from the tent.

I can never tell him what I tried to do today, because all he'll see is the money I lost. He doesn't appreciate me; he can't appreciate me. But it's not Manman's fault. How dare he say this is Manman's fault? How dare he speak her name that way! Hot tears of rage spill down my face. We are all turning against one another in this country, where the hungry steal from the hungry, the poor persecute the poor. We, the poor, on the streets, visible and exposed, with no walls or windshields to keep us safe. Everyone devours us, including and most of all ourselves.

APRIL 2011

THE NEW PRESIDENT SAYS HE'LL PROVIDE free primary school to every child in Haiti, but I'll believe it when I see it. Last night, fireworks exploded all over the Champ de Mars, but where we were, in the camp, we couldn't see them. We could only hear the thunder as it echoed throughout the bowl-shaped mountains of Port-au-Prince, and it sounded like war. I dropped to the floor in panic. Tonton Élie just said, "Mezanmi, Magda, why do you exaggerate everything!?"

I've come up with a new idea for how to make money, but it is too horrible to speak, too horrible to admit to myself, because it means I can fall no lower.

The manager of our camp is a guy named Félix Télémaque. Like most leaders, he got there because he's the one who talks the best. He knows how to tell the blans, the foreigners from the aid organizations, the sorts of things they like to hear, about hope and sustainability and making a better Haiti for himself and his countrymen. He speaks good French and decent English, and his baseball cap still has the sticker under the brim, like in rap videos. Tonton Élie says privately that he's a djolè, a bigmouth know-it-all, and a schemer. Félix is broad and muscled and a little fat. Tonton Élie says that anyone who's that fat who lives in the camp must be "drinking cool water from a nice, fresh source." Félix's belly is big, stretching out his T-shirt, and people like to tease him and say, "Oh, how many months along are you?" But they tease him in the careful, grinning way you tease people more powerful than you.

The international organization gives Félix money to pay designated people to clean the latrines, because we are supposed to be responsible for them and "have a sense of ownership." That's what Félix told everyone who went to his meeting last week. I didn't go, because kids don't go to those meetings. It was almost all men, because the women in the camp were either out selling things on the streets or washing clothes or cooking. But everyone else hears about it. People talk.

It's a joke that we should feel proud of our latrines and take good care of them. No one wants to go near them. When Nadou was here, all those pathetic things seemed funny, because I had an accomplice to go through them with. Now it's just me, and it's not funny anymore.

Félix is recruiting guys to clean the toilets, and everyone is pretty sure that he's making a little money off of it. "It's like this, Magda," explained Tonton Élie, putting his fingers together and sounding like a professor. "Say the organization gives Félix two hundred dollars a month to pay someone a living wage to clean the toilets. Félix pockets one hundred dollars and pays one of his cronies one hundred dollars. But that person doesn't really want to clean the toilets, right? You understand? It's too demeaning. So he finds someone more desperate than he is, and pays that person twenty dollars, and he pockets the eighty dollars. And then that *third* person finds someone who's really desperate, who's starving and living on their last nerve. And he pays that person two or three dollars to clean the toilet. You understand?" Tonton Élie laughed joylessly. "Everybody wins, Magda. Everybody wins."

When Tonton Élie finished his speech, I thought, *I'll clean the toilets for two or three US dollars a month.* That's about 120 gourdes, and every little bit helps. I tried to reason with myself: I'll get gloves. I'll wear a mask. I'll hold my breath as much as I can. *Magda,* I tell myself, *you're beyond humiliation. There is nothing left for you to lose. Go on, clean up other people's shit.*

I resolve to go talk to Félix Télémaque in the morning. I don't even know how I'll ask the question, though, because you can't just come right out and say that you know things don't work the way they're officially supposed to work.

I COULDN'T DECIDE WHAT TO WEAR. NORmally, if I were going to go talk to a big shot to ask a favor, I'd dress nicely, in an ironed blouse and a skirt, with earrings. But I don't want to look too pretty, or like some stuck-up girl who wouldn't be willing to clean a toilet. *This will get you to Miami,* I tell myself. *It's not who you really are.* In the end I wear a pair of jeans and a clean T-shirt with something written on it in English, and I tie a pink and yellow kerchief over my hair. No makeup. I think I look respectful and sensible—at least, I hope so.

Félix's current girlfriend is outside their door, a chunky, rounded woman in a short dress who doesn't look much older than me. She sells hot food. When I approach, she's stirring a huge pot of boiling vegetable stew with orange oil floating at the top, while an even bigger pot of white rice steams under a stretched-out plastic bag. It smells savory and spicy, divine. Manman used to have a way to describe feeling this hungry: *Your small intestine is swallowing your big intestine.*

"Bonjou," I say.

"Bonjou," she replies, not seeming very interested.

"I came to see Msyè Félix?" It comes out like a question.

"He's not here," she says.

"Oh."

"You can wait for him."

"Okay."

There's only one chair, and the girlfriend is sitting on it. She doesn't offer me anything else, so I just lean against one of the wooden poles. Félix's house is in the camp, but it's not too flimsy. He's got lots of plywood and a sheet-metal roof with new tarps over it and sandbags all around the bottom to keep the water and mud out when it rains. His tent is a lot nicer than some people's real houses.

I can't think of anything to say. *What's your name? Do you like Justin Bieber? Did you hear he is dating Selena Gomez? Who do you like more, Barikad or Izolan?* Those all sound stupid. Maybe she thinks I'm after her man? I didn't think of that. But why would he want a skinny, dried-up kid like me? But a lot of women are jealous, jealous of nothing. She ignores me. Her jeans are low, and when she leans over to check on the rice, I can see her butt crack, where her jeans gap in the back. I think she's probably showing it off—how big and healthy and pretty she is, compared to some people. She's full of juice. She shines.

I lean lightly against the pole and pretend to be busy with my phone. Actually I'm just rereading my old text messages, but at least it gives me something to do. Most of my messages are old ones from Nadou. Sometimes it's just messages from Digicel, or hand-washing messages from the Ministry of Health—I go through and delete those. *Beep. Beep. Beep, beep, beep.* I wonder when Félix Télémaque will ever come. I wonder if I can nap with my back against the pole.

It's almost half an hour before Félix strides brawnily home. There are a couple of guys with him—his deputies on the camp committee—and a whole flock of little kids, some in school uniforms, some barefoot, some in broken, oversize plastic sandals. They like him because he gives them candies or gum or a couple of gourdes. He is never not smiling.

"Bonjou, bonjou!" Félix announces as he leans down and kisses his girlfriend on the forehead.

She shrugs. "This little girl came to see you."

That's me. I'm the little girl. A wave of anger rolls like bile up my throat, but I don't say anything, even though I'd like to go at the woman's beautiful face with my fingernails. But I am here today to plead favors.

"Yes, little girl?" asks Félix in an oily voice. "Why don't you come inside?"

I follow him into the dark tent-house. It has two beds on platforms and a wooden dresser covered in makeups and powders and plastic flowers, and there's a fridge in one corner and a TV and DVD player in the other.

"Your house is very pretty," I say. He must get at least ten people coming by asking for favors every day.

"Have a seat," Félix says, and he gestures to one of the beds. It's covered in a soft blanket with a picture of a gigantic tiger printed on it. "What can I do for you, ti fi?"

"Well, Msyè Félix . . ." I falter. "My name is Magdalie Jean-Baptiste. I don't really know how to say this . . . because, you see, I'm ashamed . . ."

"Don't be afraid, little girl." Félix smiles. "I'm your friend."

He has a round baby face, despite his gold teeth, and I want so much to trust him. But I can't think of what to say next, and I just stare down at my hands, at the polish peeling off my nails.

"You need cash," says Félix. He doesn't ask. He just says it, because he knows.

"Wi," I say softly.

"And how do you think I can help you?"

I still my heart and think of Nadine. I think of how soon we will be together, far away from here. All it will take is for me to push through this, through the stench and the heat, through the humiliation, and on the other side will be Miami and Nadou.

"I heard—I mean, I thought that maybe I could help clean the . . . the toilets."

Félix looks at me for a moment. Then his wide face breaks into a smile like a cleaved pumpkin, and he begins to laugh. His laugh is deep, boiling out of his mouth.

"Oh, little girl, that's a good joke. That's a beautiful joke!"

"But . . . I'm serious."

He just laughs harder. "I see you're serious! That's why it's such a good joke!"

"I'm a hard worker," I insist. "I'm stronger than I look. I never get sick. I'm not afraid of working."

"Why would a pretty girl like you want to clean toilets? Are you crazy? Are you a crazy person?"

I gulp. "I need the money, like you said."

"Haven't you heard of cholera?"

"I'd be careful."

"Listen to me, cheri. You go out and find a man to screw, a cock to suck. You're a very pretty girl. Lots of guys would give you money, give you food. I'm just explaining it to you logically, like a businessman. I'm a businessman, tande—you hear me? And you're not thinking logically."

"No," I murmur. "No, that's not for me . . ." My eyes are hot with tears that I can't allow to fall. I can't let Félix think of me as even more of a scared little girl than he already does.

"Eh, bien," he says. "Ah, well. Deal with it. But you're not cleaning those toilets. It's for your own good, little sweet thing."

His voice is firm, like a father's might be, only it is dripping with sex.

That's it. I can't argue. "Mèsi."

"Come back and see me when you're ready to start thinking logically," he says. "Like an adult."

I leave, and the girlfriend says nothing, just stares at me as I go. The sun is blazing, and if I go back to the tent, I'll get cooked under the metal, so I just walk and walk so I can be alone and maybe think. I am thirsty. I wish I could buy an icy Coke from the lady with the cooler on the corner, but I don't have twenty gourdes. *How thirsty would you have to get, Magda, before you'd suck a zozo for that Coke?* I ask myself, and I hate myself for asking the question, I hate myself for wondering.

Is there nothing else for us? I'm seething. Is there nothing else young women can do than sell our bodies and our youth? *I am sorry, God, for judging them. For judging girls like Safira. We're all one illness, one hunger pang, one need away from being Safira. From being the beautiful girls in their tight jeans and their long, straight weaves and their shiny lips, haunting the Grand-Rue, prowling the street corners of Pétionville at night, aglow in the fluorescence bouncing off the wet black asphalt. I'm sorry, Manman, if I can't think of any other way.*

I was wrong, before, when I thought that cleaning the toilets was the worst thing that could happen. You can always fall lower.

I GO HOME AND PLAY SNAKE ON MY PHONE in the dark until the battery dies. I can't concentrate, anyway. Félix Télémaque's words stick in my mind like black burned rice on the bottom of a cooking pot. *A man to screw, a cock to suck.* I don't have anybody to talk to, but I need to talk to somebody.

The next morning, after I make coffee for me and Tonton Élie and wash last night's dishes, I cross the camp and rap on the sheet metal of Safira's door. I hear a child crying inside.

"Cheri!" exclaims Safira as she opens the door, a wet-faced little boy on her hip. "How are you, boubou?" She gives me a kiss on the cheek. "This is Christopher, my auntie's little boy. He has a fever today and couldn't go to school." The little boy stares at me, tears hanging on his lashes, and he hides his sticky face against Safira's shoulder, smearing snot on her sleeve.

Safira looks me up and down. "Why are you angry? What's wrong? Something is wrong with you. Come in and tell me."

I sit on the cot. "I tried to get a job yesterday."

"For real?" She sits down, the little boy balanced on her lap, his hot cheek resting against her pregnant belly, and rocks him. "What about selling the water?"

"You were right. It wasn't safe. So yesterday I asked Félix if I could clean the toilets."

"*Woy!*" exclaims Safira, and she begins to bubble with laughter. "No, no! Are you serious? You're serious! Wo-o-oy, Magda!"

"I have to make money somehow!"

Safira shrugs. "That's because you don't accept your situation."

"I'm swimming to escape."

"Ah, my friend, you can't deny God's plan."

The little boy, Christopher, has fallen asleep with his mouth open, snoring in a wet, congested way, like a piglet. Safira hoists him up over her shoulder.

"I'm going to drop him off at the neighbor's so I can go get some asòsi leaves to boil for his fever. Come with me?"

"Okay." Before he left this morning, Tonton Élie gave me fifty gourdes to buy beans and a little cornmeal. Safira drops the sleeping, feverish little boy off with a lady selling sodas from an Igloo a couple of tents over

("Mèsi, cheri, I'll be right back"). We start up the hill to the street market.

"Eh, bien," Safira says, shrugging. "What will you do now?"

"I don't know," I say.

One of the plastic straps on Safira's sandals is broken, and it flaps around, making her limp and drag in the dust.

"These damn cheap things," she says.

"Manman used to wear sandals called Ti Fanfane. She said the mountain women like them because they never break, even in the mud."

"Do they sell them here?

"I think if you go downtown. They sell them in all sorts of different colors."

"They have purple?"

"Probably."

"How much do they sell for?" Safira asks.

"I'm not sure . . . maybe seventy-five, one hundred gourdes?"

"Well . . . I don't have that. Not today, anyway."

"I think I've got an extra pair of plastic sandals at our tent." They are Nadine's old sandals. She'll never need them again. "I'll give them to you when we get back."

Safira smiles her wide, trusting smile. "Mèsi, cheri!"

"Pas de quoi, ma chère, not at all, my dear," I reply, as aristocratically as I can manage, just to tease. Safira laughs, and I'm suddenly aware of how comfortable and familiar her presence feels. Is Safira my friend?

"Safira, do you ever worry about the future?"

"I think about the future. But I trust in God. It's all in His hands."

"I know, but . . . Sometimes I feel like I can't control anything. I keep trying to get someplace, but I never arrive. I never, ever arrive."

Safira rests a bony hand on her belly. "The baby just kicked." She giggles. She looks down, speaking to the child inside her. "You're dancing konpa already, pitit mwen? You're already dancing?" Then she looks back to me. "Magda, you know the preachers say that suffering is part of life. To be a good Christian, you are supposed to suffer, and we should accept it. God knows what He is doing."

"My uncle says that's a god of poverty and misery. He says the blans and the preachers taught us to believe in a god of poverty so we wouldn't complain."

"But God didn't create poverty, Magdalie. We did. Man did."

"But God created man . . ."

"In any case, we can only control what we can control, right?"

Safira possesses so much peace. I don't think I could, if I were in her situation. But she radiates peace, like warmth. Does she really feel so secure, so certain? I have no right to doubt God's plan, but I feel that I can't believe in anything anymore.

A huge truck chugs down Route Delmas, belching a cloud of pure black exhaust into the air. Little boys gather on the median, asking for coins, trying to wipe down windshields. They know better than to ask the white UN and Red Cross cars, though. Their drivers will never give them money. A young man on Roller-blades hitches a ride up the hill by holding on to the back of a truck.

"Why don't you ask that guy to lend you some money for your plane ticket?" Safira asks suddenly.

"What?"

"That guy, the boyfriend of your cousin."

"Jimmy? I can't!" I exclaim. "Not after I borrowed that money for the water and never paid him back. I think he hates me."

"I don't think he hates you. Maybe he'd understand. Is he a good person?"

"I think he's a good person . . ."

"If he's a good person, then he'll understand," Safira decides aloud.

"I'd be so embarrassed. I'm ashamed."

"Look, Magdalie, you say you want to go to Miami."

"It's not just *want*. I *need* to go."

"Then *ask* him. Ask him! There's nothing to lose, right?"

"No . . . The worst that can happen is he'll say no, right?"

Safira nods, her black eyes wide. She looks a little sad. She sighs and slides her hand back and forth across her swollen belly.

I can't just wait for my fate to happen to me. I'm not a thing, like a rock or a bucket or a tent or whatever that can just sit around all day not caring what happens to it. I have to keep moving.

"You have to put every drop of energy into finding a solution, Magda," says Safira. "Do it for me, because I can't."

"Chouchou . . ."

"Ask your cousin's boyfriend. If he loved her, he'll do it."

Safira's idea is making more and more sense to me. "Jimmy does have a job, and his papa is in New York, and he sends Jimmy money every month. He's got a car and a camera; he buys his clothes new."

"He's got money!" Safira exclaims. "He's loaded!"

"That money I owe him for the water—that can't mean much to him. He doesn't *need* it. And when I go to Miami, I'll get an education and a job and make money, and someday I'll pay him back for everything."

I summon all my courage, like an invisible jacket that will protect me from humiliation and judgment, as if I'm so hardened and burnished now by everything that has happened to me that I've become invincible.

MAY 2011

I'M GOING TO GO AHEAD AND ASK JIMMY IF he can lend me more money. Safira seemed so full of faith that things would work out. I don't have enough money left on my phone to call him. I just send him a pre-programmed "Appellez-moi s'il-vous-plaît" message and wait for him to call me back.

The phone rings an hour and a half later, as I sit in front of the tent, picking tiny rocks out of rice spread out on the table and flicking them into the dirt. "Wi, Magdalie!" Jimmy says. "Sorry I didn't call right back; I was in my word processing class."

"It's no problem, no problem. How are you?"

"I'm fine. And you and your family?"

"We're all fine. Listen, Jimmy . . ." I don't know how much money he has on his phone, so I don't want to keep up the small talk too long. "Listen, there's something I want to ask you about. But I'm a little embarrassed."

"You don't need to be embarrassed, cheri. Just ask."

I clear my throat. "Things have been hard lately. I told you Tonton Élie says he can't pay for my school. I don't know what to do. I can't stay here anymore. I need money so I can go to Miami and be with Nadou."

"What about the water? I thought I lent you that money to sell water."

"I . . . I was too ashamed to tell you. Thieves took the money. They pulled a gun on us in the taptap, and then I got too scared to ever go back again. I'm sorry. I should have told you, but I was afraid you would get angry."

"Pòdyab, you poor thing." Jimmy pauses. "You need money?"

"Wi. Nadine's supposed to be working on getting me a visa." I'm dizzy with expectation.

"It's no problem, Magdalie. Of course it's no problem. You're Nadine's little sister, okay?"

I exhale. It's as though someone has just taken the weight of a bag of cement off me. I could take off and fly. "Oh, thank you, Jimmy. Thank you, God! Thank you infinitely!"

"Can you come meet me tomorrow afternoon? There's a little resto a couple of blocks in, in Delmas 33. I think it's called Gloire à Dieu."

"Yes, yes, yes, yes! Of course! Thank you, thank you, Jimmy!"

He laughs. "Magdalie, it's like you're my own little

sister. Of course I'll help you." He hangs up, and I think: "Mèsi, Jezi, at last, something is going right."

Every afternoon, it rains. Hurricane season is beginning. The sky boils gray with clouds, then the rain falls in quivering sheets, and the city disappears. Our tarp roof leaks, but by now I know where to place the buckets to catch the water, until they overflow and we run out of buckets.

All the walls throughout the city are still covered in rows upon rows of identical posters bearing the grinning faces of presidential candidates, peeling off, fading, and defaced, from December's election. I have to dance around a couple of machanns selling mangoes, papayas, and passion fruit on the wet, filthy sidewalk, to climb the narrow mosaic stairs to Gloire à Dieu bar-resto. I'm a few minutes late, but Jimmy isn't there yet. No one is there. It looks like the kind of place that gets little business during the day but becomes a discothèque at night. The walls are painted in neon swirls, the ceiling dripping metallic garlands and crêpe-paper coils. In a corner, a small grainy black-and-white TV plays *Pirates of the Caribbean* for no one.

I sit on the edge of a white plastic chair, my back straight, not removing my purse. I don't even have enough money for a soda, and I'm afraid I'll get kicked out. I take out my phone: no missed calls, no message from Jimmy. After a while a chubby young woman in plaid shorts comes out of the kitchen, drying her hands on a towel.

"Can I help you with something?"

"No, thanks . . . I'm just waiting for someone."

"Okay," she says. "We don't have any food right now. But we've got drinks."

"Okay. Mèsi."

She disappears into the kitchen again, and I turn to the TV, where a giant squid is destroying a ship. Jimmy is now twenty minutes late. A slow dread begins to creep over me that he might not come at all.

But then he appears in the doorway, full of apologetic smiles. Jimmy doesn't show his teeth when he smiles, making him seem shy. "Magdalie!" he cheers, and he gives me a hug and a kiss on the cheek. "How are you, ti cheri? It's been a long time since I've seen you! You don't have to worry anymore. I'm going to fix all your problems." He gazes around the room. "But let's go somewhere more private."

That makes sense. You don't bring out a lot of money in public, certainly not in the middle of the street and not even in a mostly empty restaurant, because someone could always see you. I follow Jimmy through a dark hallway and down another set of cement stairs. "Do you come here a lot?" I ask.

"Sometimes," he replies. "I come here sometimes to drink a little rum and enjoy myself." As we hurry down the stairs, he puts a hand on my waist to steady me.

"I'm all right." I laugh. "My feet have roots. I won't fall."

We arrive in a lightless little room with a tiny window set higher than my head, facing into an alleyway.

"Thank you again so much for doing this, Jimmy," I repeat. "I don't know what I would have done. Sometimes I feel like I have no one left."

Jimmy smiles and gathers me in his arms and calls me sister. It doesn't feel like the kind of hug a brother would give his sister, but I don't try to pull away. He is very warm, and he smells like cologne. "Ti Magda," he murmurs, "I'll take care of you." His hands slip under my blouse and up my back.

"What are you doing?" I ask. I hear my voice as if from far away, as though it isn't coming from me. I sound too calm.

"Come on, Magdalie." His hands unhook my bra, then slide down to the gap at the back of my jeans. "You look a lot like your sister."

These jeans were always too loose, I think. *I knew I should have worn a belt.*

His zozo is hard and swollen and hot against me; I can feel it through his jeans. All my mind can come up with is a bunch of words with little thought attached to them: *Heat. Closeness. Zozo. Cologne. Sweat. Dim gray sunlight.* No emotion or thought, only panic. *Run. Run. Run.* Music from the TV blares through the building, reaching us where we are—rollicking adventure-movie music.

"No, Jimmy. Please," I whisper. "I don't want to do this." I try to push him away lightly, hoping that what's happening isn't happening, that it's all a joke, that I might be misunderstanding it all.

"Come on, Magdalie, my Magda," Jimmy says again, his voice higher than usual. "Don't be stuck-up and cold like your sister. Come on. I thought we had an agreement."

He leans against me, and his tongue penetrates my mouth, quick, muscular, and slippery. His beard stubble stings my cheeks. Jimmy makes a noise, like a growl or a grunt, deep in his throat. He clasps me tightly against him. I hold my breath. My mind starts to float away to a safe place, far away from my body.

It wouldn't be so hard, I think. *A few minutes, and then you'll have everything you need. You'll go to Miami. You'll have Nadine back. You'll have everything you need. You're the only person you can rely on, Magdalie.* I keep my mind focused on that distant place, far away from the gray bar-resto and its dim back room, beyond those wrought-iron windows garlanded with dusty cobwebs. Somewhere safe, where there is no pain and no shame.

This is easy, so easy. Jimmy begins to fumble with my zipper. He pulls my jeans down to my knees. He slips his finger inside my yellow cotton kilòt. *Easy.* He licks his finger and slips it inside of me.

We bought these kilòt when Manman took me and Nadou shopping for school clothes downtown in August before our first year of high school. A new school year meant new panties, a new backpack, new pencils.

Jimmy is sweating. I feel the clamminess of his palms as he runs his hands over my hair. The pinkie fingernail of one of his hands is long and pointed, so he can pull the SIM card out of his phone. Drops of sweat gather like blisters along his hairline, on his upper lip. "Magda," he murmurs hoarsely.

Once I start thinking about Manman and Nadou, I can't get my mind back to the safe, faraway place. I try to force it back, but I can't. I can't get Manman's voice out of my head. *Listen, pitit mwen yo, my little ones. Whatever you do in life, don't beg. No matter how hungry you are. And don't ever sleep with a man for money.* She used to tell us that, me and Nadine. And we'd laugh at her, because it was such a silly thing to say, because we weren't beggars or whores.

Come back, Magdalie. Don't lose yourself, Magdalie.

Jimmy's mouth is sour and frothy; it tastes like stale kleren and pineapple candies. "Come on, Magda," he sighs. "You owe me this."

I want to be the person you dreamed I would be, Manman. Manman, Manman, I want you to be proud of me.

"No!" I cry, and I pull away, pushing Jimmy as hard as I can, with all my rage, with the rage of a hundred girls. My nails scratch trails into his forearms. "Don't touch me anymore!"

He looks shocked, confused, and hurt. "You're the one who wanted this."

"That's not true!" I scream, pulling my jeans back up.

"What a freeloading little slut you are, Magdalie!" Jimmy roars. "You think people will just give and give and give and never ask anything in return?"

"Go fuck yourself, Jimmy!"

He lunges at me then, clenches my wrists in his hot hands and pins me against the gritty, cold cement wall. "Don't scream, Magdalie, or I'll hurt you worse."

"Don't do this," I whisper, and I try to twist out of his grip.

His lip curls. "Your plan is idiotic," he breathes softly over my face. "Your plan is the plan of a stupid, naive child. You are never going to get to Miami. You think Nadine can get you a visa? She couldn't if she wanted to. And she doesn't *want* to. Nadine has moved on. Nadine doesn't care about any of us. Nadine doesn't care about you."

Jimmy lets me go, then spits at me. That sound contains all the hatred in the world. I run, pounding up the gray, dark cement steps, dashing through the empty restaurant and slipping on the wet, cracked mosaic stairway. I run as if a demon is after me, until I'm delivered back into the bustle of the street market of Delmas 33. I'm shaking all over, but I keep walking as fast as I can. I'm too furious to cry. I can't remember the last time I cried. *He's right. Nadine has forgotten me. There's nothing left for me. There is nothing left to hope for.*

Maybe Jimmy is right about me, too. *Freeloading little slut, you think people will just give and give and give . . .* It's true, it's true, I'm always looking for an opportunity or a handout. It's true.

It starts to rain, and the rain feels good. As the machanns look for cover and pull all their pèpè off their hangers, and as all the other women pull out plastic bags to cover their hair, I keep walking. *I'm sorry, Manman. I'm sorry, Manman.* I feel like a crazy person, and I know I look like one. I walk straight through the rain, through the puddles and the mud, all the way home.

I NEVER TOLD TONTON ÉLIE ABOUT WHAT happened with Jimmy, because it was too shameful. I am so stupid for not having known that would happen, for having ended up in that situation. And I was ashamed that I almost had sex for money, even if I didn't do it. I feel dirty and frightened every time I think of the smell of cologne and the feeling of Jimmy pressed up against me. How could I ever tell my uncle that? It's not the sort of thing you can tell a man. I've got it sealed up in my heart.

I don't even tell Safira.

"What happened with your cousin's boyfriend?" she asks when she comes by to borrow a bit of detergent.

"It didn't work."

Her eyes grow hard. "What did he say?"

He said the ugly thing that I fear the most. "He said, um . . . he said he didn't have the money."

Safira gazes at me as if she knows I'm lying, but she doesn't say it. Instead, she says, "Do you believe that?"

"Does it matter?"

"Hmmph!" she says, leaning against the door frame. "Men. Liars, vagabonds."

"All of them?"

"Mmm. Not all. But plenty. They'll tell you sweet words, they'll call you cheri doudou, but as soon as you give them what they're after, it's a hit-and-run. They turn around and get out of there."

"Is that what happened . . . ?" My gaze falls to her pregnant belly.

"He said he loved me. Used to sing me love songs. Said he would always be there for me. Ala traka, what can you do when you fall in love with a liar?" Safira laughs, but her eyes look sad.

"Do you want to come in?" I ask. "We have a kowosòl. It's ripe. I could make juice."

"No, no, I have to wash all this laundry before my auntie comes home. Just— Magdalie?"

"Wi?"

"Just like how I put too much trust in that guy . . . Maybe you shouldn't put too much trust in your cousin."

"My *sister.*"

"Your sister. Maybe she . . . maybe she isn't able, or she doesn't know . . . I don't know."

"You don't know what you're talking about, Safira!"

I snap. "You don't know Nadine. She wouldn't do that. You don't know anything."

She nods. "You're right. I'm sorry. It's not my business. I'd better go do my washing."

I've stopped having patience for anyone. Other kids in the camp playing soccer and being loud make me angry. The rap and bachata that fill the air and pierce the tarp whenever the electricity comes on fill me with hate and make me bury my head under the pillow and curse them in my mind. It is so very hot under a tarp roof. My dreams awaken me, exhausted, aware, and furious.

I used to cry, but I can't now, ever since I realized that Nadine had let me go. I want to scream and scream and scream enough to split the sky in two, but I choke whenever I try to weep. I feel as though my head is expanding sideways, ready to explode.

Every day I have waited for her. Because she promised, because a sister wouldn't make a promise and then forget about me. Every day I have waited for her call: *Magda, cheri, it's time. I arranged your visa. Go to the embassy. I've fixed everything.*

It's an effort to drag myself out of bed each day.

I am washing clothes when the blan comes and takes my photo. It doesn't surprise me. Foreigners take a lot of photos, and sometimes Haitians do, too: of the rows of temporary toilets and of people collecting water. They take photos of children, sometimes the clean ones with neat hair but more of dirty kids with no pants. They take photos of amputees, like Noémie, who lives on the other side of the camp, not realizing that she didn't lose her leg in the earthquake but in a traffic accident six years ago. They take a lot of photos of rubble and of tents and houses made of tarps.

When the white man in the baseball cap takes my picture, I've got my skirt tucked up between my legs so it doesn't get wet. I'm sitting on a low wooden bench, leaning over the plastic basin of soapy water, washing underwear. I'm humming the song from the Whirlpool commercial. The camera is black and huge, like a wide, fat gun. The man sweats greasily and smiles as he bends down to take my photo.

No one likes having her picture taken while she's doing chores and a mess. I'd rather put on a Sunday dress and get my hair permed and put on some lip gloss and be standing in front of something nicer than a tent.

A memory flickers across my mind—something I haven't thought about in months. A few days after the quake I saw a foreign photojournalist setting up a shot. He had an assistant with a big pointy black umbrella and lights, and he was taking a photo of a man sitting on a big pile of rubble. *Now, why is that idiot sitting on a huge pile of rubble?* I'd wondered. It didn't make any sense to sit on top of a pile of rubble in the bright sunlight like that. There were other places to sit. And then I realized that they had *put* him there for the picture.

Now, with this new photojournalist crouching down, his knees cracking, his camera trained upon my face, I remember that scene in the rubble with the posed man.

I can't stop laughing. I laugh in a crazy, desperate, too loud way that seizes my whole body. Tears roll down my face and my throat fills with phlegm. And I think, *Nothing is funny, nothing at all. Nothing will ever be funny again.* But I cannot stop laughing.

The photojournalist takes my picture—skirt tucked up, hands soapy and wrinkled. Sweat turning to salt rings on my blouse. *Click, click, click.* I look down and see that my knees are grayish, and I think that I should put on some lotion. *Click, click, click.* The camera's shutter opens and closes like a knife slicing against stone. I'm laughing so hard, I can't breathe; my chest is in spasms.

The photojournalist has thin, almost invisible lips pursed in graveness, a narrow nose, and a plump double chin. His hair is hidden under his baseball cap. His face flushes pink in the tropical heat. His eyebrows are knit into a practiced gaze of compassion and pity. He says something nasal in English to his Haitian translator. The translator leans toward me.

"He says, how wonderful it is to see you so happy and laughing. He says he loves the light in the eyes of the Haitian people, your resilience, in spite of all your suffering."

A scream rises from me like a searing vapor, but I do not hear it. I dimly glimpse the sudden fear and shock on the face of the photojournalist as I hurl my basin of dirty washing water at him, the thud of hard plastic against his shins, but the expression and the sound mean nothing to me. Someone utters a vulgar curse against the photojournalist's mother, and I don't comprehend that it is me. If Manman were here to hear them, those words would have earned me a beating. I am bursting out of my own skin. I do not think in words; I only feel a shapeless desire to tear and to destroy.

Safira appears—I don't know from where—and seizes me by the arms, apologizing to the photojournalist and his translator in self-conscious, flawed French. "Désolée, désolée. She's having a crisis. She doesn't know what she's doing . . ."

She guides me through the camp, and pushes me into her own tent. She has me lie down on the bed. I still can't breathe—my breath comes in jagged, high-pitched wheezes, and my head rolls from side to side. My heart thrums hard in my chest. I wonder, *Am I dying?* Safira unbuttons my blouse and pours a little bag of treated water over my face. "Okay, doudou. Don't excite yourself, ti kokòt . . ." She hums a hymn as she sits on her heels in the corner, boiling leaves and soaking dishes in an old yellow Ti Malice bucket. Tears run out the corners of my eyes, dripping into my ears, and after a while my heart grows quieter. I begin to feel embarrassed.

Safira pours the hot tea through a strainer and hands me a steaming cup. "We boil this where my family is from in the Artibonite," she says.

"Us too." It is verbena tea, and it makes me think of Manman and how she'd boil verbena tea whenever someone was angry or shocked. I don't know what else to say to Safira. I want to apologize for having acted the way I did, but I can't find the words. I stare at the swell of her belly. However ashamed I am of what Jimmy almost did to me, I am relieved not to have let him get anywhere near my bobòt. Safira sings softly as she washes the dishes, and her voice grows louder with each line. It is unexpectedly beautiful and clear—such a strong sound from a seemingly weak body.

Dieu tout puissant quand mon cœur considère
Tout l'univers crée par ton pouvoir,
Le ciel d'azur, les éclaires, le tonnerre,
L'éclair matin ou les ombres du soir
De tout mon être alors s'élève un chant . . .

And when she gets to the final line of the hymn, I mouth along,

Dieu tout puissant, que tu es grand!
God Almighty, how great thou art!

Safira pauses as the final note vanishes from the air soundlessly against the dull tarp walls. She keeps her eyes on a fixed spot, looking neither at me nor at the dishwashing in front of her. Her thin hands with their long bones work as though they have memorized the chore.

"I told you before that my manman sent me here when I got pregnant?" she says suddenly and softly.

"Wi, I remember."

The water splashes as she scrubs a blackened pot with a scratching sound, and she hums the final line of the hymn again. "But that's not the whole story. My manman was sick. They said she had tuberculosis. Some people were talking; they said it was a curse, and she must have AIDS. The hospital gave her medicine, but we didn't have any food. And I had to take care of her."

I stare at my hands. I feel light-headed and drained, as though maybe this is a dream, and Safira's words just keep coming, running over me like water.

"The guy, I told you, who said he loved me? He told me he'd give us food vouchers and money if I slept with him," says Safira tonelessly, still not facing me. I count the bumps of the vertebrae on the back of her neck.

I remember again what Manman always told me and Nadine about men. We'd laughed! We were so naive. Manman had sheltered us. She'd taken the blows of the world for us. Poor Safira, who had had no one to keep her safe.

"Did she get better, chouchou?" I ask. "Did your manman get better?"

Safira looks up at me and smiles. It's the first real smile I've seen on her face, as though all her other smiles were false. A wide smile, with her one crooked tooth, a smile that transforms her face and makes her glow. "I saved her," she says softly. My head feels heavy, and I turn my face to the wall and fall asleep to the *scratch, scratch* of Safira scrubbing.

It's dark when I wake again. The light is on, and a moth skitters against the bulb, making weird shadows on the tarpaulin roof. I think of the demons who stalk the night. Outside, I hear hushed voices—Tonton Élie and gossipy neighbors—fragments of sentences, bits of words floating like ash and dust in the wind.

"It's not normal . . . ," says Jilène, our neighbor who does pedicures under the tree.

"I don't know what to do," replies Tonton Élie.

"Seek a remèd for her anger . . . ," declares someone else, whose voice I don't even recognize, someone nosy.

"She's sleeping now." That is Safira's voice, firm and practical. "She can stay tonight."

It is sweet and easy to lie there. A strong wind is blowing; somewhere, a loose tarp flaps, like some great bird taking flight. Somewhere, an evangelical pastor bellows into a megaphone, and his congregation thrills, *Thank you, Lord! Thank you, Lord!*

I think: *I'll never get up again.*

THE AIR IS SWEET WITH THE SMELL OF CINnamon and star anise as Nadine deals the cards onto the table. We hunch in plastic chairs, socks on our feet and sweaters over our pajamas, as we shiver gratefully near Manman's hot charcoal stove; it's an uncommonly cold winter morning. Manman stirs plantain porridge, pours in a can of Carnation milk, and I can hear Nadine's stomach growling in anticipation.

We play Casino as we wait. We've been playing with this old, ragged set of cards for so long that it's easy to cheat—you can always tell who has the seven of diamonds or the ten of spades because of how the corners are folded—but it's not fun if you know what's in the other person's hand, so we pretend we don't know at all. It is dark and cozy in the downstairs kitchen because there's no electricity this morning, and I feel warm, sweet, and peaceful, as if I've just drunk a cup of thick hot chocolate. I am relieved, and I can't remember why I should feel relieved—only that there was once a sense of danger but that it doesn't exist anymore.

"Krik?" says Manman.

"Krak!" Nadine and I call back in unison.

"What's a tiny little thing that can make the pride of the president?" asks Manman.

"A needle!" I shout.

"A needle to make his suit!" shouts Nadine.

I throw down a queen and use it to pick up a nine and a three and put them in my pile. I am winning. My pile of cards is growing.

I never win at Casino. Nadine reaches out suddenly and grabs my hand.

I feel frightened. Why are you holding my hand? *I want to ask.*

I'm falling.

I'm falling. Then it is dark and unfamiliar. I'm lying on a strange canvas cot with something lumpy under my head. For a moment I want to scream. I don't know where I am. Then I see Safira, sleeping on the ground, snoring softly, the sharp angles of her elbows and knees atop a tangle of sheets. *That was a dream. This is what's real now.* I feel sadness and betrayal in my chest, as if something beloved and comfortable has been ripped out of my hands. I close my eyes and try to go back to dream-Manman and dream-Nadine, but I can't. I try to force time to go backward. *Don't go, don't go, please don't go.* I grind my teeth into the hard, lumpy pillow, and I don't cry. I keep smelling cinnamon and star anise as I stare into the corners where the tarp is nailed down, where darkness distorts the shapes of things, and I wait until morning.

Sunlight seeps through the thin plastic walls. A rooster crows, and a machann promenades boiled eggs and ripe bananas: *"Ze bouyi fig mi! Ze bouyi fig mi!"* I sit on the cot; my body feels old, as if all my bones are rubbing against one another.

As Safira makes coffee, she begins to tell me her story.

"I won't tell you his name," says Safira softly as she runs sweet coffee slowly through the strainer over and over, until it's black. "He was a leader in the Cité, down on Route Neuf, and I knew if I got in good with him, everything would be okay. He'd fix everything for me. Manman wasn't getting better, and the neighbors started telling me it wasn't a natural disease. They started telling me it was a sent disease, a curse. And the nurse—the nurse was so mean! She said it was my fault that Manman needed to eat good food with lots of energy and iron. And I didn't have cash. I didn't have anything to sell."

"But you managed. You got by."

"He said he loved me. And I thought he did. I thought it would be okay if he really loved me." She pauses. "You know, I was a virgin before that," she says with a smile.

"You saved your manman."

"Yes. And she was so angry when I got pregnant. I never told her why I did what I did. She would have been ashamed."

"Are you ashamed?"

"I'm not ashamed. I'm not ashamed." Safira runs her hands over her hair, then ties it up in a pale orange kerchief.

"That's good."

"But I don't know what to do. You fix one problem, and another one comes up. Both my feet are in a single shoe. What will I do with this baby?"

She stares at me, as though she expects me to really answer her.

"I don't know," I say at last.

She looks like a child now, wide-eyed and young, soft and believing. Everything she has done, she has done to protect the ones she loves. Jealousy creeps in and gnaws at me. Because, amid all her suffering, there are still people in the world whom Safira loves. Her heart isn't hard and angry. She's not like me.

JUNE 2011

TONTON ÉLIE SAYS HE'S BRINGING ME TO the manbo—the vodou priestess—for a cure because I've become so angry. He's been saying it ever since I attacked the American photojournalist last month. He says I'm lucky I didn't get arrested. It is embarrassing, but I can't hide that I still feel that the guy deserved it.

My sandaled foot sinks into black ooze as Tonton Élie and I push and elbow our way toward the taptap. Around us, every day is a market day, and a painted placard in front of the big stadium advertises an upcoming match between Valentina and the Tigresses.

"I wonder what it would be like to be a girl soccer player," I say. I'm trying to be friendly, not angry or sad, even if I feel angry and sad.

"They're all lesbians," murmurs my uncle, the vertical lines between his eyebrows severe. Then he pauses. "You want a Tampico?"

That's not like him, to waste fifteen gourdes like that. He must be feeling bad for me.

"The pink Tampico," I say, and he puts two fingers in his mouth and whistles for the young man selling cold drinks out of a cardboard box balanced on his head. Then we get onto the crowded taptap to Martissant.

The road to the south, the one that takes you through the sprawl of the Martissant shantytown and beyond, all the way out of Port-au-Prince, is always dusty (except when it rains, and then it's muddy) and always full of traffic. We're squeezed into the taptap, seven people on each side, and I'm at the front, my feet resting on the spare tire. A younger and an older woman stand hunched under the low ceiling. They are carrying chickens.

"I lived in Martissant when I first came to Port-au-Prince," Élie says suddenly, over the churning of the engine and the throbbing bass of the speakers.

"I didn't know that."

"My brother Benisoit knew someone. So that's where I went." Tonton Élie pauses for a moment and then starts laughing. "There were so many cars. When I got off the boat and made it downtown, that's all I could see—so many cars, half of them going one way and half of them going the other. I said, '*Woy!*' I didn't know what to do."

I try to imagine Tonton Élie as a young, naive man arriving in Port-au-Prince from the provinces. I can't imagine him wide-eyed.

Élie's smile disappears, like a startled cat into the shadows, as quickly as it came. "We were looking for a better life," he says quietly. "Look at what we've got."

The manbo, Manman Niniz, lives in a pink two-room cement house down by the sea at the outer edges of Martissant. It's also where she works her cures and does her ceremonies. A small stripy gray cat is curled on the porch. It mews at us boredly with a candy-pink tongue. We sit in white plastic chairs and sweat.

"What is the problem?" asks Manman Niniz. She is a short, expansive woman with soft-looking dark skin. She leans on her wooden table, which is covered with peeling images of the saints and the lwa, the vodou spirits. Off to the side stand a bottle of Florida Water perfume and another of Bakara rum and a few half-burned candles. A machete leans against the wall, its point in the dust.

Tonton Élie rests his elbows on his knees, his chin on his hands. "This is my niece. She has too much kolè. She is full of anger."

I am a burden to him. He never wanted me. I had two mothers in my life, and both of them died. There is no one to love me.

Manman Niniz takes my hand and looks into my eyes. When she leans close, I smell cigarettes and see a few coarse white hairs at her temples and a few black hairs on her chin. "My child," she asks, "why are you so angry?"

I am surprised to hear my own voice saying things

I have never said aloud. "Because the world is bad. Because people are suffering—because good people are suffering. Because of the earthquake. Because the earthquake killed my manman. Because Nadine . . . my sister left and forgot about me." And there are things I am still afraid to say—that I thought Jimmy was my friend, but he thought I'd have sex with him for money, and I nearly did . . . that everyone always says, *Bondye bon! God is good!* But sometimes I wonder if He really is . . .

The anger boils inside of me. The earthquake broke open all the sadness in my heart, and I could only patch it up again with hardness. I took my fear and my sadness and turned them into hate, because it made me feel strong instead of weak. I never want to stop feeling angry; I can't afford to feel anything other than angry.

I say quietly, "I wonder if God has forgotten us."

Manman Niniz knocks twice on the table, then closes her eyes. Beads of sweat glisten on her forehead and her upper lip. Low-pitched sounds, halfway between a hum and a groan, escape her mouth, and she lets go of my hand. She drops her head, shakes it back and forth a few times, and then sits in silence.

I've been to lots of ceremonies before, but I've only been to one healing—when we were little and Nadine had typhoid fever, and Manman took us to an oungan who told her to do an offering for the Marasa spirits, who protect children. But all I remember from that is that Manman cooked a lot of food, and then a bunch of kids came to eat, and then we wiped our fingers on the oungan's clothes. I've never seen anybody be cured of rage before.

When Manman Niniz opens her eyes, she looks like another person—she has been mounted by the spirit Gede, who stands at the crossroads between this world and the afterlife. She widens her eyes, so I can see all the white, and she peers at me with seemingly mocking fascination. She rises, lifting her skirt around her thighs as if she's trying to seduce a man, and ties a shimmery purple kerchief around her fleshy waist. She sways to the table and picks up a bottle of kleren with scotch bonnet peppers in it and pours a little onto the dirt floor, in the doorway, then takes a swig. She daubs her face with talcum powder. Then she sticks out her right hand, then her left hand, to me for a brisk double handshake.

"Well, my child!" Manman Niniz intones in Gede's nasal voice. They say Gede talks that way because he is dead and his nose is stuffed with cotton. He is the master of the cemetery, master of the underworld. *"Don't you think I'm bweautiful?"*

"Wi," I tell the lwa. "You are very beautiful."

"You twell me you are too angry."

"That is what everyone says."

Manman Niniz/Gede calls out, *"Marie-Georges! Come here!"* A few moments later, a small woman all in white steps in from the lakou. She is an ounsi, one of Manman Niniz's followers. *"You, go with her,"* commands Manman Niniz/Gede, gesturing to me. *"Your uncle will stway here to discuss the pwayment with me."*

Marie-Georges takes my hand (hers is as hard and callused as leather) and leads me out of the dark wooden house and into the sunlight. We walk through a few neighbors' yards, past a charcoal-colored bristly piglet eating sweet-potato peels out of a plastic bag, to the swampy marshland that separates the city from the sea.

"How are you today?" I ask, because I don't know what else to talk about.

"Very well, thank God," replies Marie-Georges, smiling. She is old enough to be my grandmother, but she has beautiful straight white teeth.

"My name is Magdalie."

"Take off your shoes, and roll up your pants," says Marie-Georges, removing her own sandals.

I take off my flip-flops and roll up my jeans to just below the knee, as high as they will go. Then I follow Marie-Georges into the water. It is filled with rusting tin cans, discarded shoes, and other floating debris; soft fans of green and brown algae sweep back and forth in the gentle current. The rocks beneath my bare feet feel slimy and slippery. The mud squishes, cool between my toes. The water soaks the bottoms of my rolled-up jeans, and I know it's filthy, and thoughts of cholera flit across my mind, but I don't say anything—I don't want Marie-Georges to think I lack courage.

We reach an outlying bank—soft, sandy earth where low, scrubby plants grow. Marie-Georges leads me to one of the bushes. "Pull up some of this," she instructs me. "Wake it up." I do so, and we walk a bit farther, and Marie-Georges gestures to another plant. "Now pull up some of this. Wake this one up." I do so, we move on, and she gestures to a third plant. "Now, tell this one why you need it, and then pull."

"I am too angry," I say quietly, kneeling down and holding the tough, ropy shrub in my hands. "Since Nadine left, I am angry all the time." And I pull.

Marie-Georges and I walk back to Manman Niniz's house under a wide blue sky. A distant white helicopter stirs the air, its propellers in the shape of a blinking black cross. *UN* is written on its white belly.

Back in the house, the spirit Gede takes the plants from my hands and twists them. *"Now we will braid them togwether."* I braid one end while Gede braids the other. Gede looks me up and down, as though the spirit suddenly recognizes me, and touches my leg softly. *"Oh, I swee, Dantò walks with you."*

My eyes fall to the table where Ezili Dantò's image sits among some of the other lwa. She is a dark-skinned woman holding a child—like a brown Mary, with three cuts on her cheek. A jewel-studded crown blossoms from her head like a flower, and she has a narrow nose and a small delicate mouth. Her deep, serious eyes peer out from a blue, red, and gold cloak. She holds the child like a devoted mother. She is beautiful and scarred, like my Manman, who served her.

Marie-Georges comes in from outside with a heavy rock from the water and places it in my hands. The rock is slippery, gritty, and dark, like a bruised organ. Gede places the braided bundle on the floor, next to the burning candle and the 250 gourdes Tonton Élie has paid. I don't have time to wonder where he got it. *"Now, pitit mwen, hit the plants—turn thwe rock and hit them three twimes and twell them your problems."*

I concentrate on the braided bundle of stems and thorns, trying to send everything I feel into them. I turn the rock in my hands. "I can't stop being angry." I slam it down the first time.

Again I turn the rock in my hands. "I hate everybody. I hate everything. Nadine said she'd send for me, but she never calls. She never calls at all." I slam it down a second time.

I turn the rock. "Please. I don't want to be in the world sometimes. But I can't be like this anymore. Help me." I slam the rock down and leave it there.

"Now you must get these things," Gede says. *"An image of Dantò, a bottle of rum, a bottle of Florida Water, a red kwerchief, and a machete. Put the machete and the kwerchief under your bed, and leave them there. Come bwack in three days."*

I DON'T DREAM THE FIRST NIGHT AFTER MY visit to Manman Niniz; I sleep a restful sleep that I cannot remember. The next day I go downtown to the Grand-Rue. I go over to Safira's tent and ask her to come with me, but I don't tell her what I'm going to buy. "Some things I have to get in Lavil," I tell her vaguely. I don't like going downtown alone now.

"Lavil? I could pick up some lalo leaves," Safira says brightly. "I've been craving it. Lalo with rice and salt beef! I don't want the baby to get a birthmark if I don't get what I crave."

So we take a taptap downtown. Playing hopscotch around the mud, garbage, and puddles in the street, as Nadou and I used to do a long time ago, we duck past the machanns selling hair extensions and boxes of relaxer, past the plastic bucket of turtles (pets or food), past the savory-smelling flat baskets of dried djondjon mushrooms. There are baskets piled high with sweet spices and fresh bergamot, medicinal leaves and edible leaves, white American rice and expensive yellow Haitian rice that no one can afford. There is a rainbow of beans and peas, both dry and fresh. Papayas, mangoes, passionfruit.

"You know, Magda, it's not true, what they say."

"What's that?"

"There's not a food shortage in Haiti. There's a *money* shortage." Safira laughs.

While Safira heads to the vegetable machann and haggles over her lalo, I make my way to where they sell things for ceremonies. There are multicolored powders and colognes for sale and little cloth dolls in tiny chairs for making someone fall in love with you.

"Oh! Mezanmi!" Safira comes over to me, holding a black plastic bag of lalo leaves. "I didn't realize we were buying things for devil worship today." But there's a teasing tone to what she says.

"What religion are you?" I ask.

"Catholic?" she replies vaguely, in the way that really means "a little of this, a little of that."

While Safira hovers nearby, cautiously running her thin fingers over a sequined bottle with the skull image of Bawòn Samdi, I negotiate the price of a machete, red kerchief, and image. The vendor is an older woman without a lot of teeth and with a pipe in her mouth, both of which make it hard to understand her. I like her because she seems strong. The red kerchief is satiny.

The queenly image of Dantò is the same one I saw at Manman Niniz's house.

Soon we're squeezed back into the taptap, facing each other and hardly moving in the traffic up Route Delmas, when Safira suddenly inhales sharply. "Oh!"

"What's wrong?" I ask, terrified that the bumpy road has made her go into labor.

"Look!" She points out the wooden slats, out onto the street. I turn around. Everyone in our taptap turns around.

They are breaking down a camp. I can't see who "they" are—if they are police or agents from the mayor's office or agents from an aid organization. They are men, I can see, muscled, their skin wet with sweat, in matching white T-shirts.

"Oh, no . . . ," says Safira softly. "Oh . . ."

The men have sticks and hammers. One of them shouts, "Break 'em down! Break 'em down!" The tents and little shacks crumple easily into the dust. The people stand there, holding whatever they can, as the sun beats down. An old man with a cane. A young man in long jean shorts with a radio in his hand. A little boy wearing a backpack, holding a pack of crackers. A young woman, her hair wrapped in a lace scarf, leaning against a woman who might be her mother. A little boy clings to an older girl's skirt with both hands.

"He's looking at me," says Safira.

"What can we do?" I ask.

"We can't do anything."

Safira and I are silent, tired, and lost in thought the rest of the way up Route Delmas. Her pregnant belly looks all the more swollen upon her skinny knees as she sits on the hard wooden taptap bench. I lean my forehead against a rusted beam. For some reason, I think: *I want to live forever*.

As we walk back down to the tents—slowly, for Safira's sake—she asks suddenly, "Do you think there are lwa who can protect my baby?"

"I think so. If you serve them. You should go talk to a manbo or an oungan."

"I know," Safira says quietly. "I just don't have very much money or very much to give. I don't want to make any promises I can't keep." She pauses. "You know, I'd give my own life to make sure that my baby had a good life. If someone could guarantee me that . . ." She looks so sad for a moment. "Where will those people go?"

"I don't know. They'll go somewhere."

"I'll bring you some lalo and rice tomorrow, once I've cleaned and cooked it," Safira says. "I'm not sure if I'll find any salt beef."

We reach the camp. Some little boys are playing soccer, and a breeze caresses my hair like cool fingers. Safira says, "It's beautiful," and she is right: our camp is beautiful, framed against the dusk, in the darkening pink of the hazy sky.

THAT NIGHT, AFTER I PUT THE MACHETE with the red kerchief around it under the bed and the image of Dantò under my pillow, I have a dream that begins like a familiar nightmare, until it changes.

I am trapped in a shaking house. The floor lurches like a boat on a stormy sea. I know if I do not get the door open soon and flee, the roof will collapse onto me. I fumble with the lock, unable to get it open. I am not able to scream or move or say a word.

I feel something around my ankles and look down. It is a pool of blood, washing up against me, hot, rising, and frothing. I look up and see Dantò. It is not the Dantò of the image, with her fine cloak and jewel-encrusted crown. But I know instantly that it is Dantò before me. She looks like a peasant woman in a dark blue denim dress. She has a beautiful, wide face and black skin, and her head is wrapped in a red kerchief. Deep, horizontal wrinkles are carved into her forehead, just as they are carved into the foreheads of all the market women who carry heavy baskets on their heads all day. Her eyes burn with fury, devotion, and heartbreak. No sound escapes her lips. She opens her mouth, and blood pours out. Blood pours from the three cuts on her cheek, but she never falls. I know that Dantò is holding the shaking house up with her strength.

I look down and see my own blood running down, but it doesn't make me feel afraid. The hot, rusty scent of it rises to my nostrils. I just think: I endure, I endure. *I look mutely at the lwa, and the lwa stares mutely back, her eyes aflame with all the anger and love the world can contain.*

"Manman," I say with sudden recognition.

With a single push, the door flies open, and I escape into the world.

When I return to Manman Niniz's house in Martissant at sunrise three days later, I come alone; Tonton Élie is out looking for work, like he does most days.

"Pitit mwen," says Manman Niniz as I enter. "How are you feeling?"

"Not too bad," I respond, leaning down to kiss the manbo on the cheek. She still smells like cigarettes and burned kleren. I open my mouth to tell her about my dream, but then I don't—I won't tell anyone about it, not even Manman Niniz. It's a secret between me and Ezili Dantò. If I speak about it, I might spoil what Dantò has done for me.

Manman Niniz knocks twice, then places the bottle of rum I've brought on the altar and lights a candle. She has boiled the now-dry braided leaves together into a dark tea, and pours in some Florida Water perfume. She has me strip down to my panties and instructs me to stand in a metal basin, and she begins to pour the liquid over me as her followers look on. It feels cool over the tiny heat pimples that itch and prickle on my back, and it smells like the forest and the sea, like flowers and spicy orange—like the Haiti of imagination, the Haiti Manman told stories about, that existed before the cities and the dust.

The three ounsis dressed in white sing songs I do not know, songs of love and pain, songs that our ancestors sang, songs that survived slavery and the passage across the sea, songs that outlived death.

Words dance and fill my mind as I close my eyes and accept the coolness of the liquid running over me, running down me like blood. *The world deserves our anger. We should be angry at the injustice and the loss.*

"*Ke-ke-ke-ke-ke-ke!*" cries Manman Niniz, eyes blazing, as wordless Ezili Dantò takes control of her body. Dantò lights a Comme-Il-Faut cigarette and holds it in her lips as she continues her work. The ounsis' song rises, they cry *Ezili, o!* in the rum-colored candlelight, as the cigarette smoke swirls and dances up to the ceiling.

I let my head fall against my chest as the liquid cascades down my neck. *We should be angry for everyone who never had a chance, for everyone who searched for life and only found suffering or death.*

Ezili takes the bundle of leaves in her hand and rubs my body down with fierce tenderness. I envision all of my sins, all of my anger, all of the poison within me being scraped off and washed away.

We should be angry for everyone who was born strong and able to love, and who then became hardened and shut off and allowed the love in her heart to be leeched out and slowly replaced by anger.

And I begin to cry—not the tears of anger I have shed in frustration and shock since January 12, not the tears of bitterness that I have shed since Nadine left—but tears of grief. My grief pierces me like daggers. My memories pierce me. The tea hangs like dewdrops from the tips of my hair. I want to be an angry, avenging woman. I want to vomit blood.

We can be our own protectors. We must love ourselves as our own mothers would love us. Our mothers want us to be at peace. The world deserves our anger, but we owe it to ourselves not to hold the anger in our hearts.

Is there hope? I ask.

There is always hope, answers a voice, which may have been my own but may not have been. *There is never certainty, but there is always hope.*

I stoop down, put my arms around my knees, bury my head in my arms, and rock myself back and forth like a child in her mother's embrace.

JULY 2011

SAFIRA WENT BACK TO HER MANMAN IN Cité Soleil. It was a few days before I noticed. I'd been experimenting, trying to make coconut tablèt candy, and I wanted to bring her some. It was ugly, ugly tablèt; when the sugar hardened, it stuck to the plate with whole pieces of cinnamon still lodged in it. But it didn't taste too bad. I went to her tent, but I didn't find Safira. The plywood door was padlocked.

"She's gone," said a young man in the neighboring tent, peering at me as he scrubbed his sneakers with detergent.

"Where?"

"To Cabaret. She should be back tomorrow morning."

"What? No, not the aunt. I'm looking for Safira."

"Oh, she's gone, too. She left."

"Where did she go?"

"Who knows?"

"Oh. Okay."

I can't let myself feel sad. People disappear so suddenly. I was just getting used to her. I take out my phone and call her. It rings and rings, and I'm about to hang up when I hear a distant *"Alo?"*

"Alo? Safira?"

"Magda!" It sounds as if she's shouting from far away.

"You didn't tell me you were going!"

"Bon. Chouchou. I was afraid to tell you. I wasn't even sure, you know, until it happened. My manman didn't want me in the camp anymore. She heard they are tearing down the camps."

"So you're back in Cité Soleil?"

"You know, things aren't so bad in the Cité now. It's not so dangerous, like it was. And none of us can stay in the camps forever."

"You never said good-bye!"

"I hate saying good-bye!" Safira cried.

"You'd rather I get sezisman, that I die of shock when I find you gone?"

"I'm sorry, cheri m nan! Really!"

"Okay," I say. "When will I see you again?"

"Don't worry, cheri! You can come see me whenever you want!" she insists, and then my minutes run out, and the call drops.

She's right. We cannot stay in the camp. None of us can. The little bonds and communities we made will have to come apart. *Safira,* I wonder, *what will you do now?* What if she never comes back? What if I never see her again? Her image suddenly conquers my mind. Her narrow chest, her jutting limbs, her stupid, trusting smile. Her sacrifice laps at my heart, menacing the dam against my emotions, threatening to overflow. Safira, who saved her mother, who saved her family. I've never known such jealousy. I imagine her and her act, and for the first time since before the earthquake, I pull out my journal and write.

Safira, full of love, wordlessly pressed her arm over her eyes, the crook of her elbow sticky over the bridge of her nose. She did not cry out. She breathed through her mouth, submitted her body, and let go of her mind. Her body remained, but she was not there. She kept a part of herself sacred and whole. Her soul, like a frightened bird released from a pair of cupped hands, flew away. It was not there. It was not in that room, on those sun-dried sheets smelling of bleach, in that room that smelled of sweat and sex. It could not hear grunts or whimpers. It could not feel pain. It slipped through a crack in the front door, out into the bright sunlight. It ascended, higher and higher. It flew over Cité Soleil, beyond the abandoned sugar factory, buffeted by the wind, until the shanties and cinder-block houses and garbage-filled swampland were just a distant, jagged pattern like broken pieces of glass. It flew over Port-au-Prince once, circled, and then soared out over the bay and up into heaven.

I could not hold on to Nadine. I cannot hold on to Safira. All I can do is hold everyone in my heart, the only place I know where I can keep them safe.

AUGUST 2011

MICHLOVE HAD HER BABY BACK IN THE provinces, Tonton Élie told me today. They didn't even have time to get her all the way down the mountain to the clinic in Abricots. She ended up pushing out that baby right on the banks of a stream. It's a little girl, and they've named her Kethly Yolène. The "Yolène" part is in memory of Manman.

"Whatever her name is, I'm going to call her Ti Ravin—Little Stream," I tell Tonton Élie. "I heard of someone who gave birth in the taptap on the way to the hospital, and they called the baby Little Truck. Mezanmi, Michlove gave birth at the stream." I can just see it. Michlove's a fat, strong, juicy girl; she'd have no problem giving birth. I suspect that Yolène a.k.a. Ti Ravin simply fell out of her.

"Very funny, Magdalie." Tonton Élie doesn't look up

as he screws together an old TV set. "You know, life is going to change for you soon."

"Of course it will, uncle-of-mine." What a stupid thing to say. My life has never stopped changing lately. That's all life is made of: change. Nothing stays.

"We're going to have to move out of the camp soon."

"I know."

Tonton Élie puts down his screwdriver and looks me in the eye. "I have to go to Jérémie in a few days. I think you should come, too."

"Me, Tonton? I don't even remember the provinces. What would I do there?"

Tonton Élie leans back on his heels. His rubber sandals are worn through at the soles. "There are a lot of people back there who would like to see you. It would be good for you to leave Port-au-Prince for a while."

"Yeah, but, Tonton, someone has to stay here and take care of the house—what if it rains? Who's going to catch the water?"

"Listen, Magdalie." He clears his throat. "I shouldn't leave a sixteen-year-old girl alone for that long. All the brothers and sisters have been putting some money aside for Yolette's final prayer and wake."

"Ah. I understand." I can tell that Tonton Élie feels nervous telling me this, because his forehead looks as creased and complicated as the circuit boards he is always fixing.

Manman always used to talk about how someday she'd go back to Jérémie. At least for a visit, and maybe forever, to build a house and start a garden.

When she'd made enough money, when she finally had the means—she'd go home. It was one of her many dreams that would never come true.

"You should come," says Tonton Élie, gazing at me seriously. "I think you should come. Just for two weeks or so. You can stay with Tonton Benisoit and Tati Marie-Lourdes."

I don't say anything. It feels wrong that this is the reason we're going back to Jérémie. Manman is supposed to be here and alive, and Nadou is supposed to be here with me, and this should be a happy trip. I shouldn't be burying Manman. I pick at a scab on my knee and don't pay attention to Tonton Élie at all, as though I've found a hiding place out in the open.

"Magdalie," he says. "*Magdalie.*"

"Wi, tonton."

"Will you come?"

"Ça va, tonton."

"It might be hard, you know. People will cry and fall down. But you are strong."

Am I? I wonder. But I don't say anything. I would rather hide.

"I wouldn't tell Nadine the same thing," Tonton Élie continues. "But you've always been stronger than she is."

Could that be true? I'm as flexible as a reed, who can bear any weight and never break? I'm strong enough to withstand the ceremonies, the crying, the remembering, but Nadine isn't? I've always been the louder one. Maybe she ties up all her feelings and swallows them.

TONTON ÉLIE DUG MANMAN'S BONES UP from the shallow place they buried her after the quake, near Mme Faustin's house, where Manman died. I hadn't gone there before because I didn't want to remember or relive the earthquake or run into Mme Faustin.

I'd imagined a dry and dusty mound, but the ground over where Manman was buried was covered in flowers, growing and blooming. There was hibiscus everywhere, and orange-red blossoms; the ground felt moist, and the air smelled like frangipani.

"It's a miracle!" I told Tonton Élie.

He looked at me with his mouth twisted, as if he wasn't sure whether he should speak. "No, Magdalie, not a miracle."

"Of course it's a miracle. All these flowers . . ."

"Mme Faustin stops by to tend them."

I stared at him. "That's not true."

It's not true because I hate her. I never want to see her again. It's not true because I refuse to believe it, because I know what I know: that she is nasty and disgusting and cruel. It's not true because it was her house that Manman died in.

"You think things are simple!" Tonton Élie exclaimed.

"How can *I* possibly think *anything* is simple?" I snapped back.

He shook his head and said, "Sometimes things are more complicated than they seem."

I looked at him hatefully. There was nothing to lose. I'm too old for him to beat me.

"Think about it, Magdalie. Use your brain. Who took care of Madame Faustin when she was sick? Who bathed her? Who fed her?"

"Manman."

"Who cooked for her, every single day? And brought food to her on a tray when she couldn't get out of bed?"

"Manman."

"Who slept on the floor of Madame Faustin's room, listening to her cry when some boyfriend had left her or one of her children was in trouble in New York?"

I sighed. "Manman."

"Who was there, in Madame Faustin's house, every single day for almost twenty years?"

"My manman."

But that doesn't change anything for me, even if Mme Faustin loved Manman in her way. What kind of love is that, where you pay someone 1,500 gourdes a month to break her back and call it charity? Manman may have been Mme Faustin's best friend in the world, but Mme Faustin was never Manman's best friend. I'll never, ever believe it.

"Rayi chen, di l dan li blan," said Tonton Élie. "You hate the dog, but you have to admit that it has beautiful white teeth. You may hate her, Magda, but you can't make yourself blind to what is good."

"I'm going home," I told him. I didn't want to talk about this anymore. And I didn't want to see the shovel hit the bones. I didn't want to be reminded.

It was Tonton Élie and two neighbors who'd found her, two days after the quake. There wasn't a mark on her, they'd said. Not even the polish on her toenails was cracked. They had wrapped her in a sheet and buried her shallowly in the unmarked ground.

Still, we are lucky because we found her, because we knew where she was buried, even if we had done it fast and with no funeral. I saw in the newspaper that in the treeless mountains beyond the city, there are mass graves of the unknown, unclaimed dead, tens of thousands of jumbled, nameless people, marked with plywood crosses rotting in the rain. In collapsed buildings throughout the city, there are people still buried.

As for Mme Faustin, she escaped without a scratch. She was born lucky. She came to see us only once after the quake. She spent the whole time crying, and I thought she was showing off. She never came back to see us or to help us again. So I know, I know I am right to hate her.

SEPTEMBER 2011

THE FERRY TO JÉRÉMIE ROCKS IN THE darkness, still tethered to the wharf, as the rain falls and the bay surges. I sit on the floor, my head resting on my knees, my eyes closed, feeling the cold rainwater seeping into my jeans. I check to make sure my cell phone is safe and dry in its plastic bag. I'm miserable, frightened, and already seasick, and we haven't even left Port-au-Prince. I sing to myself some song I heard on the evangelical station so I will feel less alone: *Advesè m kanpe, yo kanpe pou m pa pase* . . . My adversaries stand before me, they stand and impede me . . .

When the storm clears and the stars come out, the boat at last begins to move. We will travel all through the night and reach Jérémie after daybreak. As we pull away from the wharf, I start to cry. My chest is tight. I miss Manman even more right now. It has been almost two years since we lost her, but in this moment the wound feels fresh and raw.

Élie brought Manman on the boat last week, in a plain wooden coffin. He is out in Jérémie already, making the preparations. We will bury her in the land she grew up in, and for nine days we will perform her denyè priyè, her last prayers.

I barely know St. Juste, the tiny village in the mountains near Jérémie, the place where I was born. I left when I was just a baby. I haven't been there in years, not since I was a little tiny child, and never without Manman. I've got a bunch of cousins and aunts and uncles there, but I don't know them very well—they are distant childhood memories and half imagination. I'm going to stay with Matant Marie-Lourdes and Tonton Benisoit, and I'm worried I won't recognize them when I see them. I wish Nadine was here. I wish Safira was here. I just need someone in the darkness with me. I take out my phone from its plastic bag, and I send a text message. IM SAD NADOU. I WISH ID NEVER GOTTEN ON THIS BOAT. I feel a little better just for having sent it, even if Nadine doesn't write back.

Everyone is talking, jokes and chatter, politics and gossip. Some women are singing and praying. To my left, a young man takes occasional sips out of a Roi des Coqs rum bottle he's carrying in his pocket.

On the floor next to me, an older man with a kind, lined face and several missing teeth pats his leg and says, "Go ahead and lie down, cheri." He must see how tired I am. His voice reminds me of Manman's accent, and I lay my head down and, breathing in the dusty scent of the man's work trousers mixing with the ocean breeze, feel myself being rocked to sleep. Suddenly I feel very, very tired, as though all the exhaustion of the last year and a half has descended on me all at once, making me sink like a stone into sleep.

ST. JUSTE IS ON THE TIP OF HAITI'S SOUTHern peninsula, as far from Port-au-Prince as you can get. After the overnight boat trip to Jérémie, you get off at the wharf, where people are selling sweet cinnamony coconut konparèts and cold sodas. Then you take a moto-taxi for an hour and a half, over rocky mountain roads, to Abricots. It is a clean little town where the sea crashes against the sandy beach, which is strewn with discarded conch shells. Then you walk up another mountain for two hours to get to St. Juste.

They send my cousin Jonas and another teenage boy to fetch me in Abricots and help me carry my bag up the mountain. I don't recognize either of them, and if Jonas remembers me, it was as I was when I was three. But when they see me getting off the moto in the town square, Jonas immediately calls, "Magdalie?" Maybe they know me because I look like someone from Port-au-Prince, or maybe because I look confused, or maybe because I look like Manman.

"Bonswa, kouzin." Jonas grins. "We're so happy you're here."

"Mèsi, kouzen." I feel shy.

"I'm Mackenson," says the other boy, leaning in to kiss me on the cheek. He is tall and wiry yet muscular, with clear, soft-looking skin. I can tell he's been swimming from the salt crystalized in his hair.

"Magdalie," I reply.

"Let me carry your bag," Mackenson says, and he tries to take it from my shoulder.

"I can do it," I declare proudly. "I'm not a child. I'm as strong as any boy."

Jonas laughs. "It's not because you're a child or a girl, no? You're not used to it here. You're not used to these mountains."

"I walk all over Port-au-Prince. The sun here is no hotter than the sun in the city."

But the mountain is steep and full of rocks and thorns. Sweat drips, stinging, into my eyes. My calves burn and ache. I fall behind but am too hardheaded to say anything until I lose my balance and put my hand down on a thorn.

"Can it be my turn now?" asks Mackenson, and he hoists the bag lightly on top of his head.

We climb the mountain as though we are ascending through a painting. The red cracked earth beneath our feet, the wide blue sky brushed with white clouds stretching out over the dark sea, the coconut palms as dense as a carpet in the valley below. How could I have been in Port-au-Prince just yesterday? Now I am at the last limit of the earth.

"Magdalie's got a thorn in her hand!" announces Jonas as, at last, we trudge up to the house.

"Oh no!" frets the woman who must be Matant Marie-Lourdes, jumping up from where she sits, peeling breadfruit. She wipes her hands on her skirt, her wide warm face pinched in concern. "Oh, mezanmi, the poor little thing hasn't even gotten to the *house,* and *already* she's hurt!" She turns to Jonas ferociously. "What were you *thinking?*"

"I'm fine. It's nothing!" I insist.

She clucks. "Let me find a needle to dig it out."

People keep apologizing to me, at first. "You know, we don't have much here," they say shyly. They think that coming from Port-au-Prince, I'm used to luxury—even though they should know better. "We're poor, chouchou," Matant Marie-Lourdes tells me anxiously, her hair wrapped up in an old T-shirt on top of her head. "We live in the middle of nowhere. It's not a very big house. Our floor is dirt. I hope you don't get diarrhea. I hope the water doesn't make pimples pop up all over your skin."

"Matant mwen, what kind of girl do you think you're talking to? I sleep in a tent," I reply, and I start laughing, and she does, too. Because what is she apologizing for? She might say it's the middle of nowhere, but to me, St.

Juste looks like paradise. There are trees, trees, trees as far as I can see, and a shimmering ocean brighter blue than a Samaritan's Purse tarp.

Tonton Élie looks like a different person here, freer and looser, as if someone has squeezed all the tension out of him. The big ropy veins in his forehead don't pop out anymore, and he smiles and laughs more. He doesn't look as thin. "Here, I am myself," he tells me. "I can fish. I can swim in the ocean. If I am hungry, I can just go hit an avocado out of a tree or climb and get a coconut. The only thing we don't have here is money."

Tonton Élie holds his little Yolène in his lap, giving her huge open-mouthed grins.

"Gaaah!" she squeals, and she emits a clear stream of drool. He holds her to his chest as if she is the only treasure he will ever need. I look into her shining black eyes, the little innocent, and I wonder what life will bring her, what God has set aside for her.

Everyone on the mountain knows who I am, but I don't know who they are. Whenever I walk by a house, the people in the lakou call, *Oh, Magda*-lie*! Come, let me look at you. All grown up! How are you? Koman kò a ye?*

"Magdalie! Oh, how you look like your mother!" coos an old woman I don't recognize, taking off her straw hat and standing on tiptoe to kiss my cheek. She starts to cry, tears falling from her white lashes.

"Please, please, Auntie," I say. "You don't need to cry, please."

Maybe my being here is finally making everything real for them. I'm a living connection to Port-au-Prince and the devastation they have heard about but haven't seen. And I remind them of Manman; my presence makes her loss real. I am here because she isn't. I am here in place of the person they knew and loved.

After a while the days begin to blend together, and without realizing it, I start to feel as though this is my new life. St. Juste is a different world, so quiet and sweet. Sometimes the earthquake seems like a nightmare from which I've awoken, and Port-au-Prince feels like someone else's life. For brief flashes I wonder, *Was there really ever an earthquake? Was there really ever a Port-au-Prince?* And then I run my fingers over the fading scars on my knees and remember, and I try to picture Manman's face.

I spend afternoons dozing on a straw mat outside the house, helping my little cousin Béatrice make dolls out of banana stalks, braiding hair, and having my hair braided. We play oslè, hopscotch, with a smooth set of goat bones, and even though Béa's hands are tiny, she is so much better at tossing them and picking them up. I bathe with my girl cousins in the shallows of the warm sea, and then we jump into the cool river, scrubbing each other's backs with a lacy old pair of panties that makes our skin smooth.

Slurping okra sauce and tonmtonm with salted fish in it, eating until sleep clouds my eyes, I remember, but can no longer feel, my old gnawing desperation and sadness. My cousin Joanne laughs, her amber eyes crinkling, as I pick up a gob of tonmtonm with all five fingers.

"Just use these two, ti kokòt, my sweetheart cousin!" she says, pinching together her index finger and thumb. And the whole family says that even baby Béa, who is only four, can swallow bigger pieces of tonmtonm than I can.

I sleep in a bed with Joanne and Guylène, and sometimes Béa gets in, too. The bed is made of slats of wood covered with lumpy old clothes and rags with a sheet over them. The slats of wood are balanced on old empty USAID vegetable-oil cans, and sometimes in the middle of the night they slide off, and the whole bed collapses on one side. But I can't complain, even if my back aches, even if we keep falling down, because everyone else in the family is sleeping on the floor on sisal mats. Everybody is so kind to me, but I wish they would stop treating me like a guest.

"I'm going to get water," announces Joanne one afternoon.

"Let me go with you," I implore as she starts off barefoot toward the river with two five-gallon empty buckets.

She looks doubtful. "I don't know, Magda . . . Do you think you can do it?"

"It's not that far! And I carry water all the time in Port-au-Prince."

"But you know there are mountains here . . ."

"Stop treating me like a child!" But that's ridiculous—children carry water here all the time. "Stop treating me like I'm not *family*!"

Joanne relents, handing me one of the buckets. As we

walk to the river, the sticky mud clings to the soles of my flip-flops. Joanne picks a mango off a tree and starts to peel it with her teeth as she walks.

"Do you have a boyfriend in Port-au-Prince?" she asks.

"No . . . not yet."

"There's no one you like?"

"No. I'm not interested in that."

"Oh! Magda . . . Everyone is interested in that!"

"They're all the same. They'll tell you nice things, they'll call you ti chouchou, they'll say, Je t'aime, but none of it's true. They're all only after one thing."

"And what's that?" asks Joanne, teasing.

"Pussy."

She pauses for a moment. "Well, they do like that," she says. "But there are good guys and bad guys. Maybe you'll find a little boyfriend out here!" She giggles, sucking the fibrous mango pit and casting it into the trees.

When at last we climb the hill down to the river, we go to a spring hollowed into the rocks, where Joanne uses her bucket to take out all the old water filled with silt and leaves. The water slowly fills up again, while a rock-colored crab scurries from crevice to crevice.

"There used to be a water pump up the mountain," Joanne explains. "But it stopped working years ago, and no one ever fixed it. The organizations don't know about it. The state doesn't do anything." She shrugs. "So we keep going up and down the mountain every day."

"You don't get tired?"

"I'm used to it."

"Do *you* have a boyfriend?"

"I had one. He went to Port-au-Prince. Looking for a better life."

Joanne fills our buckets, and we start up the mountain. It's too steep to balance the water on our heads, but Joanne nimbly ascends, the muscles straining in her slim arms and legs. I am not so nimble. The path is slippery with mud, and I start sliding backward. "I don't think I can do this!"

"Take off your sandals! Go barefoot!" Joanne shouts. "If you try to go up in your sandals, you'll fall."

I put down the bucket, trying not to slosh it all over, and slip off my sandals.

"But make sure you don't get stuck with a thorn," Joanne adds, considering. "They're hidden in the mud sometimes."

I try again, curling my toes into the mud, trying to grip, but I keep stumbling, and I'm afraid I'm wasting the water we've walked so far for. "I can't, Jo!" I squeal.

"It's okay. You're not used to it," Joanne replies, giggling as she descends, as graceful as a little bird, and picks up my bucket, too. Once we hike to the top, I'll take my bucket back and carry it on my head the rest of the way home, but I cannot do what Joanne does as she goes up the mountain, her back straight, a heavy bucket in each hand, and doesn't spill a drop. She has been doing this her whole life, walking miles and miles barefoot. This is a beautiful little world, but it is very, very hard.

ST. JUSTE IS SPREAD OUT, DEYÈ MÒN GEN mòn—beyond the mountains there are more mountains, and more mountains beyond those, with more people living on them, just out of sight.

I halt in my tracks on the narrow path between Tonton Seneren's house and Matant Jezila's lakou. There are two obstacles before me: a hulking, tawny bull with a slobbering mouth and, leading a goat on a rope, the tall, smiling boy Mackenson who helped carry my bag up the mountain. The air is warm and filled with the sweet perfume of the guava trees.

"Good afternoon, Magdalie."

"Hi, Mackenson."

He picks a small handful of ripe yellow guavas from the tree and takes a bite. The guava flesh is soft and pink, and Mackenson's mouth has an interesting shape, and his teeth are very white.

He offers me a guava. I don't move.

"Don't you want it?"

"I . . . I can't . . ."

"You can't have guavas?"

"No—I'm afraid . . ."

I must look ridiculous to him: a city girl in jeans and a rhinestone-studded tank top, standing paralyzed, her eyes wide.

"What's wrong with you?" he asks, tying his goat to a branch.

I nod in the direction of the bull grazing nearby. It flicks away flies with its tail. It looks drowsy, but you never know. "Bèf la," I whisper, afraid that the animal might turn and come if it hears its name.

Mackenson bursts out laughing. "You can't be serious."

"Bulls can kill people!"

"That old cow isn't going to do anything to you. Come on."

He reaches for my hand, still laughing. He has a high, boyish laugh, a little goofy and much higher than his speaking voice. I pause for a moment before taking his hand. His palm is rough and callused; mine is soft and pink except for the spot worn hard from washing clothes. He guides me down the path as I try to stay as far away as possible from the bored or scary cow, my eyes trained on it in case of any sudden moves.

"How old are you?" asks Mackenson.

"Seventeen," I reply. "Quel âge as-tu?" I don't know why I switch from Creole to French. Maybe I'm a little embarrassed and want to show Mackenson that I'm better than him in some way, even if I am afraid of cows. And snakes. And biting ants. And shimmery blue mabouya lizards that can jump on you.

"Same as you." Mackenson has two uneven dimples and big laughing eyes. He stands barefoot on the path. "Do you know how to eat kenèp?" he asks.

"Of course! Do you think we don't have kenèp in Port-au-Prince?"

"I was just making sure. In any case, you've never had kenèp as juicy and sweet as the ones we've got in St. Juste."

"Mmm," I reply.

"Just be careful they don't stain your clothes."

"Uh-huh."

"I could take you to the best kenèp tree right now, if you want."

"I can't—my matant sent me to Matant Jezila's to get a remedy for my sezisman."

I watch Mackenson's teasing expression soften, his eyebrows draw together. Matant Jezila is my great-aunt, a tiny old woman who knows all the leaves and herbs to boil to make remedies. I suddenly regret saying anything about shock, reminding Mackenson why I've come to the provinces at all. I see it in his face—all he can think of now is the earthquake and Manman's death, and now he's imagining what I've seen and felt and endured. I feel ridiculous, as though I'm asking for pity.

"Did you know we have a swimming pool here in Saint Juste? Have your cousins told you about that already?" One corner of Mackenson's mouth turns up in a half smile.

"I don't believe you."

"It's true!"

"You're such a comedian."

"I'm telling you the truth!"

"And you all go to the river and carry buckets of water to fill it? How can you have a swimming pool, but you have no running water and no electricity . . . ?"

"And no school and no clinic and no money!" He laughs his boyish laugh. "We have a swimming pool made out of rocks, where the sea washes in."

I can't help but laugh. "That sounds nice."

"More than nice, Magdalie. It's paradise."

"Hmm."

"I'll take you there if you want."

"Okay."

"But you should go now. Madanm Jezila is waiting for you. Demen, si dye vle, Magdalie. Tomorrow, God willing." Mackenson stoops to untie his goat and continues up the path. His footsteps stop briefly; he has turned around to watch me pick my way carefully down the unfamiliar rocky path. I pause to place each of my sandaled feet gingerly, trying not to slip. I can feel his eyes upon me, and I pray to myself, *Dear Lord, don't let me slip and fall now, or this boy is going to laugh at me forever.*

THE CEREMONIES FOR MANMAN CAN'T BE done the way we do them for people who die in ordinary ways. The rituals aren't made for people who die the same day as hundreds of thousands of other people and are tossed into unmarked, strange earth. Reburying Manman more than a year after she died is like holding a funeral, a wake, and final prayers all at once.

When people die, their souls go anba dlo, under the water, where they remain for a year and a day or longer. The dead don't like to be underwater, where it's cold and wet. The souls of the dead stay underwater until their loved ones set them free. The denyè priyè lasts for nine days, and at the end of that, we will retrieve Manman's soul from underwater; we will set Manman's spirit free.

The first day the oungan comes to Tonton Benisoit

and Matant Marie-Lourdes's house, and the ceremony begins. Matant Marie-Lourdes has made sweet, dark coffee and hands out chewy diamonds of bread. Her hair is tied up in a shiny white kerchief, and she pours a little coffee out onto the earth in front of the house for the ones we cannot see: the departed, our ancestors, and our spirits and ghosts. For a while, everyone chats, dunking their bread in their coffee and asking, "How are your children?" "How is so-and-so? I heard he had cholera. He's better now?" "Did you hear that Madame so-and-so had twins?"

I'm cradling little Yolène. A rivulet of milk-laced drool flows out the corner of her mouth. Her toenails are tiny and pink; so tiny, I can hardly believe they're real.

"Are you going to steal that baby?" asks Michlove, Tonton Élie's girlfriend and Yolène's manman.

"I'm not ready to have a baby," I reply. Of course, neither is Michlove. She looks older than she is, but she has no maturity.

The oungan, who is young and handsome, draws on the ground in white chalk the shape of a crossroads. It is Legba's vèvè—the symbol for the spirit Papa Legba, who will allow us to communicate with the spirits and the ancestors. The drumming begins, the drummer's callused hands sure and strong.

Papa Legba, ouvri baryè a pou lwa yo!
Papa Legba, open the gates for the spirits!

The drumbeat resonates deep within me; my veins

and tendons vibrate like guitar strings being plucked. As mourners enter the house, it grows hot and crowded. There are not enough chairs for everyone, so people stand and spill back into the lakou. They mostly all wear white or black.

The oungan traces Ezili Dantò's vèvè on the ground in white powder—a curlicued heart, pierced with a knife. He chants, his voice firm yet plaintive, and people join in. We dance, the women lifting their long skirts, sashaying in time with the drumbeat. I am warm, at once light-headed and grounded. My skin feels electric. The dancing lasts all morning. The drummers beat the goatskin drums until their palms are red and stinging with heat. In the afternoon, the men smack down dominoes and play Casino on old card tables. We sip kleren (sprinkling a little on the floor for the spirits) and sweet Couronne soda. After the sun sets, everyone tells stories and jokes. Manman would have liked to be here—she would have liked to sit with the people she grew up with, telling dirty jokes about the president and a donkey. I pour some of my soda onto the ground, and I stare at the dark spot in the dirt, and I remember how much Manman loved sweet things.

IN BETWEEN THE CEREMONIES AND THE obligations, we have lots of time to do ordinary things, too. Today I head down the ridge with my cousin Jo-anne to bathe in the river. Mackenson must have seen me in the distance, because he's already perched in a mango tree by the time we are about to pass his house.

"Magda-*lie*!" he calls as we walk by. His bare toes grip the sticky trunk securely, and he beams down at us from among the broad green leaves.

"Hey, Mackenson."

"Do you like mangoes?"

We enter the lakou, calling bonswa to Mackenson's grandma, who is peeling lam veritab with her grandson on her hip. "Bonswa, doudou!" she calls back as she tosses another wedge of peeled breadfruit into the pot.

"Here you go," says Mackenson, tossing several mangoes down to us and speaking in a gallant voice. "You will see they are very sweet."

Joanne and I squeeze the mangoes to soften them and release the juice, then bite them and suck, the sweet golden juice dripping down our chins. Mackenson looks pleased and proud, peering down at us from his perch, swinging his legs, but he does not descend.

"Why don't you come down and talk with us?" asks Joanne.

"Just a second," replies Mackenson, glancing around.

A wicked glimmer of realization crosses Joanne's face. "Are you *stuck*?" She elbows me. "He's stuck up there!"

"I am not! I've been climbing these trees my whole life." His feet dangle from the branch. "I'm just watching. I'm fine."

"You're not very high up," Joanne observes. "Just jump!"

Mackenson peers down cautiously, then quickly covers his hesitation with a smirk of manly confidence. "I'll jump down when I feel like it."

Joanne starts to giggle, and then I do, too. "Manmi, come help your grandson out of the tree," my cousin calls out.

Mackenson's grandmother looks up from her breadfruit and sighs, puts down the baby, then rises, briskly wipes her hands on her skirt, and goes to get the gòl they use to knock fruit out of the trees.

"Gran! What are you doing?" Mackenson yelps.

She starts poking him with the gòl as though he were a stubborn mango. Now Joanne and I laugh full on, even though I feel a little bad for Mackenson, too. He looks mortified, as though he's worrying that people can hear us laughing the next mountain over.

When the gòl doesn't work, Mackenson's grandmother rises up on tiptoe to reach him. She seizes his bottom and pushes. "Let go, Mackenson! Lage kò w!"

He grips a mango branch in panic. "*Woy!*" he yells as he slides off the branch, still hanging on to the tree with his arms. His grandmother grabs him around his waist and pulls. "Let *go!*"

I laugh so much that tears run down my face, and I gasp for breath.

Mackenson lets go and topples out of the tree and almost onto his grandmother.

"Moron," she mutters as she whacks his butt lightly.

Joanne, clasping her mango, juice growing sticky on her chin, says, "Woouch! Oh, thank you for that, Macken. Thank you for that. Oh, my stomach hurts from laughing."

"It looked higher from up there," Mackenson says defiantly.

I'm laughing so hard, I still can't speak. Mackenson looks as though he wishes he could disappear.

GROWING UP IN PORT-AU-PRINCE, YOU hear two things that don't make a lot of sense when you put them together. The first thing you always hear is that life is so much better in the countryside: you eat better, you feel better, you breathe better, you don't have to worry about thieves or political insecurity, you don't even need money because the food grows on trees. The second thing you always hear is that if you want a better life, you have to be in Port-au-Prince: if you want to be a success, if you want to provide for yourself and your family, if you want to be a modern person with education and dignity, you have to go to the capital.

Tonton Élie is peering into a piece of mirror leaning at an angle against the whitewashed wall, carefully shaving his face with a sharpened razor. Michlove went to Abricots this morning to sell molasses at the market, carrying an umbrella to shield baby Yolène from the sun. I figure this is a good time to talk, since he's alone for once.

"Tonton, I was thinking . . ." I'm trying to keep my tone as light as possible. "Maybe I could stay here in Saint Juste longer."

The razor scratches against his face. He doesn't look at me. "No."

"Why not?"

"Because I'm responsible for you now, and I say no."

"Stop talking to me like I'm a child!"

Tonton Élie puts down his razor and turns around. "Then stop sounding like a child. You come here, you spend a few days here, and you only see the good things. You think you're in paradise, don't you?"

I don't say anything to that.

"But it's because you don't know any better," he continues. "You don't see how hard life can be here, the day the crops fail, the day someone gets sick."

"Life is hard in Port-au-Prince," I counter. "You're always saying it yourself, how much you miss Jérémie and how much better life is here. How dirty Port-au-Prince is. You're a hypocrite! You always say those things."

Tonton Élie slaps his hands together, back-to-palm, in exasperation. "Of course I say those things, Magdalie. This is my *home*. Shouldn't I be nostalgic for it?"

"If this is our home, then why can't we stay here?"

"Do you want to walk three hours up and down these mountains in the sun just to go to and from school every day?"

"In Port-au-Prince, *I don't go to school at all.*"

"Damn it, Magdalie! Why does every conversation with you turn into an argument? You used to say you wanted to do something with your life, to be a great doctor or a great writer. You have to be in Port-au-Prince if you want to have dreams like that."

I feel as though I am about to cry and I don't want to cry. "You keep saying that. Everybody keeps saying that, but look at what Port-au-Prince has done to us."

Tonton Élie leans back against the wall and puts the tips of his fingers together like a professor. "Think of it this way, Magdalie. How do we eat in Port-au-Prince? I make a little money, doing this-and-that, and with the money, we buy a little food. Sometimes we get meat and sometimes we have to boil white flour into porridge, but we eat something, most days."

"*Most* days," I mutter.

"And if we really have nothing, I can go downtown and try to sell a radio. Or I can borrow money from somebody. Or I can try to get a little food on credit. You see? There's always a way to get by in Port-au-Prince. Because there's *money* there, even if we can't see it."

"But here you don't need money at all!" I exclaim. "And everybody eats. You go into anybody's lakou and they say, 'Oh, Magda, stay and eat a little tonmtonm. Here, have some fish!' You can walk around all day eating mangoes and guavas for free!"

"Everybody here eats *this week*, Magdalie. But what happens when a hurricane comes through and knocks all the breadfruit out of the tree before they're ripe? Then everybody starves, because there's nothing to fall back on. There's no big boss you can borrow from. There's nothing to sell because no one has money. There's nothing to buy on credit because no one has anything to sell.

"It's a different misery, Magda. Port-au-Prince misery and Saint Juste misery, they're different miseries. But no misery is sweet, my dear. No misery is sweet."

Every night of a funeral period is a party. You aren't supposed to come to a wake and leave hungry—or sober. And you don't need a lot of money because everyone contributes something, even if they don't have a coin to their names. Tonight Tonton Benisoit kills a goat. Matant Marie-Lourdes cooks up the blood with oil, green onion, and hot pepper and then fries the meat, makes a sauce of the tripe and chewy stomach and skin, and makes a soup from the head. Other people bring yams to boil, plantains to fry, and breadfruit for tonmtonm. The fishermen contribute some of their catch, so we have fresh and salted fish and sweet conch. Mme Ernst brings kremas, which is so sweet and creamy with condensed milk and coconut you don't realize you're getting drunk, and several old men bring plastic gallons of homemade kleren. It's enough to eat all week.

Burials are for weeping, but wakes are for laughing. The same old men tell folktales, riddles, and jokes late into the night, taking swigs of strong kleren.

Sometimes we can barely hear the stories because there is so much noise from the people playing dominoes, slapping them down, mixing them around on the rough wooden table, yelling and laughing. Mackenson is there. He is losing so badly that he's got clothespins all the way up his forearm, as punishment for his lack of skill. It looks painful. I walk over to him.

"You're pretty good at this, huh, Macken?" I tease.

The other players snort and laugh. "Macken's on another planet tonight."

He scowls. "Not true."

His older brother, Lixson, grins. "What's got you so distracted, little brother of mine?"

"I'm not distracted!"

Mackenson is so irritable that I wonder if he's still angry about the mango tree. "What's wrong?" I ask. "Why are you in a bad mood?"

He jumps a little when I speak. "No, no," he says. "Don't say that. I'm not in a bad mood, Magdalie."

Lixson takes a sip of kleren and hands me the bottle. It burns in a nice way as it hits my lips, flows down my throat, and settles like a low, warm fire in my stomach. "Don't pay any attention to him, Magdalie." Lixson punches Mackenson playfully on the shoulder, but Mackenson doesn't smile.

I walk over to Joanne.

"Why are you blushing?" she demands. "Your face is all purple and glowing."

"No, it's not."

"Go look at yourself in the mirror in the house."

"Well, you're embarrassing me!"

Joanne gazes at me appraisingly. "Do you like Mackenson?"

"Ha! What? Of course not!" I laugh too loudly, which makes everything a thousand times worse.

"Ohhhh, Magdalie likes Mackenson!" Joanne says loudly and claps her hands in excitement.

"It's not true!"

"Why are you so embarrassed? It's normal. It's natural. What, are you an Adventist or something?"

"No, it's just . . ." And I don't know how to answer. The truth is that I've been living quietly in my own head for so long now that I've forgotten what it's like to care that somebody is paying attention.

"He's a good kid," says Joanne. "He won't do anything to you."

"It's not that. That's not what I'm afraid of."

"You think too much, Magdalie. You care about him, that's all!"

But that's it; that's just what frightens me. Once you start caring about people, it matters if they disappear and don't come back.

And when Mackenson appears in our lakou the next day with four speckled eggs from his papa's chickens and says simply, without any teasing, "I brought these for you, Magdalie," there's even more to fear, because I know, for sure, that he cares about me, too.

I HARDLY BOTHER TO CARRY MY CELL PHONE here. Most of St. Juste doesn't have reception, and there's almost nowhere to charge a phone unless you walk an hour to Abricots. But today I've got my phone in my pocket, and I've got a bar of battery life left. When it vibrates against my hip, I'm momentarily confused, then pick it up, thinking it might be Safira calling.

"*Alo!*"

Static crackles over the line. At last I make out a voice. "Magda? Magdalie?"

"Nadou!"

"How are you, ti kokòt?"

"Mwen la, mwen la . . . Hanging in there." How can our conversation be so casual?

"You know what happened to me yesterday? I was

at the grocery store when I felt the earth shaking. You know how it is? And I dropped what I was holding and I just *ran* out the door into the street. I don't even remember running—next thing I knew I was out in the parking lot, and I was shaking and I looked like a crazy person. And this guy from the store came out and he said, 'What's wrong with you? You just broke a dozen eggs all over the floor!' and I said, 'Didn't you feel it? Didn't you feel it, mister?' He said, 'What are you talking about?' And I said, 'The earthquake? Didn't you feel the earthquake!' And he said there wasn't anything, and he made me pay for the eggs."

"Oh . . . And it really wasn't anything?"

"No, Magda . . . They don't even have fault lines in Miami. I was embarrassed. And it made me think of you. It made me miss you, because if you run like that in Haiti, everybody understands. But if you run like that in Miami, everyone says you're crazy." Nadine laughs. "Where are you, boubou?" Nadine asks. In the background, I hear noise like a television set.

"I'm just on my way to see Madanm Yves's second son. He has malaria, and Matant Marie-Lourdes is sending a remèd for him," I reply before I realize Nadine has no idea who Mme Yves is. "I'm in the provinces, ti cheri. Everybody asks about you."

"Oh, what are you doing there?"

"Visiting people." I can't tell Nadine what we're doing here, that we're really here for Manman's final prayers. The words rattle around emptily in my head.

"Oh, okay," says Nadine. I am the strong one, as Tonton Élie said, so I lie to her. I lie, and I have never felt as far away from her as I do right now.

"What's that I hear in the background?" I ask, to change the subject.

"*Independence Day,* with Will Smith. You should see this apartment, Magda. Papa's got a big-screen TV, but he hasn't got money for furniture yet."

"When are you going to invite me to see it?" I ask, teasing, but it's a little joke wrapped in barbed wire.

"Oh, you know . . . you know . . ." I can already feel Nadine pulling away, packaging herself up. Static howls and crackles across the line.

"Nadine, you never call. You never call me, you never call Élie, you never call any of us. We miss you, we miss the sound of your voice. I don't know if I'm coming or going. I don't know what to do."

"That's not true," Nadine says, sounding stung. "You don't know, okay? There are things . . . You know I'm far away, baby. I'll call you again demen-si-dye-vle."

There is no demen; there is only demen-si-dye-vle. There is no tomorrow; there is only tomorrow-God-willing. My whole life I've been hearing demen-si-dye-vle, demen-si-dye-vle, and I've never really thought about it. To a lady selling green peas in the market: *I can't buy any pwa frans today; I'll buy them demen-si-dye-vle, if they pay me.* To a friend: *I'll come see you demen-si-dye-vle.* I used to say those words out of habit because everyone did. Now I feel in my blood how fragile and unpredictable tomorrow is.

"I'll call you demen-si-dye-vle, chouchou," says Nadine again.

"I don't believe you." The words stun me even as they slip from my mouth, not because they're angry but because they're true. I don't believe Nadine. "You're never going to send for me. You never will."

"Don't do that to me," Nadine pleads. "I miss you. You know Haiti is my home. Please, cheri—" and then, with a *beep-beep*, her phone card ends, and the call drops.

Suddenly severed from Nadine's voice, I feel confused and unmoored, like a forgotten fishing boat bobbing in the tide. Her words ring in my ears: *Haiti is my home.* Where is *my* home? I was born in St. Juste but raised in Port-au-Prince; I don't remember living anywhere else. Port-au-Prince's streets and taptap routes and landmarks are the ones I know—even the landmarks that aren't standing anymore except in our memories. The map of the city is the map of my experience. I'm afraid of riding donkeys and mules, and I can't swim. But I've always known my people are moun Jeremi, that the foods we ate at home, the way we spoke, the place we felt we were *of,* if not *from,* is St. Juste and the mountains around Jérémie. I wonder if I, and all the other rural Haitians who had left their homes to seek a better life in the cities, have always been displaced people.

AS WE LEAVE CHURCH ON SUNDAY AFTERnoon after the regular service, Mackenson slips a folded-up piece of paper into my hand, slightly damp from his sweaty palm. I look up, a half-formed question on my lips, but Mackenson looks so shy, I don't say anything at all.

Later, after I help Matant Marie-Lourdes sweep the house, I sneak out behind the pigsty, where no one will disturb me, and open the piece of paper. It has pale lines and a serrated edge, ripped out of a notebook. Mackenson's handwriting is neat and careful, in blue ballpoint. His spelling is only so-so.

When I see you, I feel warm inside
When I see you, the planets colide
When I see you, I can't help but grin

When I see you, I am saved from my sin.
When I hear your name, it is the most beautifull word
When I hear your voice, I imagine singing birds
When you are far, I'm filled with fear
That dissapears when you are near.
I wish my fingers could be the ribbons in your hair
I wish my very breath could be your air
I wish my arms could be the belt around your waist
I wish my kiss could be the sweetest thing you taste.
You are the sugar in the papaya juice I drink
You are the happiest idea I could ever think.

Folding up the paper and slipping it into my bra, I feel the blood rise to my face. I bite my bottom lip and think of Nadine, how she would often do that, not knowing whether or not to smile.

No boy has ever really liked me before. As soon as my breasts started to grow, men on the streets in Port-au-Prince started hissing, calling me "pretty little girl" and "mi amor" and trying to give me their phone numbers. I know perfectly well what it means to be wanted for sex, but I've never had something so silly and sweet handed to me before.

Mackenson is different from the boys in the capital, who start growing up early on the streets. Boys like Jimmy. So many of them have become hardened jokers, laughing without smiling, turning their anger, pain, and disappointment into cruelness. Mackenson has innocence to him. In some ways he is like a child, but in others—his agility with a machete, a hoe, or a fishing net, and his wisdom—he's like a grown man. He is kind. I tell myself, *He is kind, Magdalie. He doesn't want to hurt you*. And he is handsome enough, with his dimples and clear, soft skin. But his ears are a little big.

I don't know what to do with this note. Half of me wants to run to Mackenson right now, and half of me wants to hide inside and never face him again. I suspect he might want to kiss me. If I went to him now, would he try to kiss me? Do I want him to kiss me?

I go back to the palm-covered kitchen, apart from the main house, where Joanne is helping her mother peel breadfruit for this afternoon's tonmtonm. "I'll help," I say, and I grab a knife. They don't know what I've got tucked in my blouse, next to my heart.

TODAY TONTON BENISOIT AND TONTON ÉLIE went fishing and brought home a basket of conch in their shells. When the lambi has nearly finished cooking in its sauce, Matant Marie-Lourdes gives me a taste. She tips the sauce and a little strip of lambi off her stirring spoon onto the heel of my palm. The sauce is spicy, salty, and delicious. The lambi is tender and sweet.

"Be careful with that lambi, Magdalie," says Matant Marie-Lourdes with a shy, knowing smile.

"What do you mean?"

"Oh, you know, lambi heats you up! You don't want to eat too much unless your boyfriend is nearby."

All my blood rushes to my face. "What do you mean, Matant? I don't have a boyfriend!"

Matant Marie-Lourdes laughs and laughs. I can't tell if she's teasing me or if she really knows something.

"Matant! Matant, it's true. I've never had a boyfriend in my life!"

As the sun dips below the sea, Tonton Benisoit bends, tying knots in his fishing net. "Do you like it here?" he asks.

"Very much," I say. "It's so beautiful. The air is so clear and light."

Tonton Benisoit nods. "This is our home. I feel more comfortable here, more like myself here, than I ever could in Port-au-Prince." He cuts the rope with his knife. "What are you going to do when you go back?"

"I am going to school, Tonton. I'm going to go back to school." My own words surprise me, but as I say them, I realize it's the only thing I want, the only thing I can want. But admitting this scares me, too, because it means coming to peace with the fact that Nadine will never send for me, at least not anytime soon.

Tonton Benisoit sucks his teeth. "I wish I could help you, Magdalie."

"I know."

"But I can't."

"I know."

"We barely get by as it is. I don't make very much money, taking the boat to sell breadfruit and yams."

"I know, Tonton. It's okay. I'll figure it out. Martelly's promising free schools. Or else I'll find a patron. Or . . . I'll figure out something. I have to." I speak with confidence I don't feel, just to reassure him. "It'll be all right."

Shadows flicker across Tonton Benisoit in the yellow light of the kerosene lamp. His hands are hard and callused, his arms covered with faded machete scars. His body is thin and sinewy, at once muscular like a young person's and buckled like an old person's. Hardship and stress age people. I've seen it all my life in Port-au-Prince, too—the swift transformation of vibrant young people to old.

What would Manman have looked like if she had been so lucky as to grow old? I think she would have been a beautiful ti granmoun.

THE SUN DESCENDS AND SPARKLES ACROSS the deep blue sea as Mackenson and I sit in the shade of his family's garden, snapping thin green kenèp skins with our front teeth and sucking the sweet pink-orange flesh off the stones, talking about nothing, making blades of grass whistle between our fingers. "Where were you, on January twelfth?" I ask.

"Playing dominoes," he replies flatly. "They started dancing."

As soon as he says this, I can see it: Mackenson and his cousins, in the shade of their kenèp tree, watching the dominoes rearrange themselves, chattering like teeth across the low table. Feeling the ground grumble beneath their bare feet. Watching the coconut palms sway.

"As it got dark, everyone stood together at the spots with the best cell phone signal, trying to call Port-au-

Prince. We ran all the way to Saint Victor." I can imagine: Tonton Benisoit sweating, his cell phone pressed against his fevered, frantic cheek, trying to get news of Manman, Nadine, and me. Matant Marie-Lourdes's long fingers worrying the fraying edges of her sisal mat as her heart pounded, fearing that we were all dead.

Mackenson goes on. "But no one could get through. The radio was just static. We knew something terrible had happened, but we didn't know what . . . We didn't know how bad it was." He pauses. "We were very afraid."

It sounds strange, but as he says that, I feel sorry for him. It doesn't seem real for me to think about what the quake felt like anywhere other than Port-au-Prince. In a place like St. Juste, on the tip of Haiti's southern, outstretched arm, is as far from the capital as you can get and still be in the country, where the quake was just a shiver.

"You know, I went to Port-au-Prince once," Mackenson announces.

"So?" I ask.

"Pòtoprens . . . ," Mackenson half sings. "I hated it."

As soon as he looks at me, he regrets what he's said. I feel my face blaze with defensive anger. "It's not that bad. There are good things there, too."

"I just mean . . . ," Mackenson gets flustered, then pauses. "I don't know what I mean."

"Oh, you're just another peasant who thinks that Port-au-Prince is a city of criminals that rots people's principles," I sputter. "You think we're all a bunch of vagabonds and thieves. But you'll have to go there someday, if you ever want to finish secondary school and go to university."

"Then maybe I won't finish school. Why do I need education? I can be a farmer." He spits a kenèp pit onto the grass.

"Don't you want a better life?" I ask.

"Port-au-Prince isn't a better life. Here, I can swim in the ocean. I can bathe in the river. I can eat my own fruit. I'm not a slave."

"Oh, you're being an idiot. You'll just end up another malere like your father and your mother and your grandfather and—and God forbid that you ever get sick, because you'll die before they can carry you down the mountain to the nearest clinic!" I hear the hypocrisy in my own voice, and part of me wants to laugh—I'm making Tonton Élie's argument all over again, and Mackenson's making mine. But something about Mackenson's disdain for Port-au-Prince makes me want to defend it—maybe not the city, but the people in it, the people who still believe in it, the people who still want to believe that it holds promise for them.

Mackenson looks angry now. "Do you really think life is so much better in Port-au-Prince, Magda? How many people left the countryside looking for a better life and have died there instead? Eh? Who's being an idiot?"

So many people from this poor and lovely mountain have gone to look for a better life in the capital: the young people who went for high school or university, the men and women who went to repair old radios and

TV sets or sell fried snacks or vegetables or pèpè on the streets . . . and people like Manman, who went to work as servants in other people's houses. They died there, never to return home.

"Here, we're never hungry," Mackenson continues. "Even if we don't have a single gourde. In Port-au-Prince, you've got to have money for everything."

How many times have I drunk sugar-water to stop my stomach from growling? I want to punch Mackenson in the teeth for being right and stubborn and wrong, but instead I seize his wrist tightly. "There's always a future, Mackenson! You can't just sit and wait for better things to happen to you, saying you'll begin demen-si-dye-vle."

Mackenson pulls me toward him; I do not let go of his wrist. "Eh, byen. Then I'll start now." And he leans into me and kisses me.

The first kiss sends a stab of breathless panic through me. I think of Jimmy's heaviness and filmy, unrelenting tongue. *This is not Jimmy,* I tell myself. *Mackenson is a good guy.* Slowly I relax a little, but I'm still nervous and self-conscious. *I'm kissing someone! I'm kissing someone!* This kiss isn't like Jimmy's. It is soft and wet. I'm aware of the kenèp fibers stuck between my teeth. The second kiss is better. I let my eyes close and let my worries and fears be carried away. Mackenson's lips are very soft and his mouth inquisitive—as though he wants to explore me but is careful not to go too far. There is no urgency and no acquisition. It's like I've just drunk something very warm, like hot ginger tea that heats me up from the pit of my stomach to my face. I hold Mackenson's bottom lip lightly with my teeth and, for a moment, have a sudden desire to swallow him whole like a snake.

Later we sit together. I rest my head on Mackenson's shoulder as we look out over the sea.

"I'll always protect you," Mackenson says suddenly. "You know, I won't let anything bad happen to you. Nothing bad can happen to you as long as I'm here." His voice is so earnest.

I squeeze his hand. "Mèsi." Just then, I love him for saying it, even though I know it isn't true. No one can control the ground beneath our feet. No one can promise to protect anyone in this world—not absolutely, not forever. But I thank him for his lovable lie.

Maybe . . . maybe that's what Nadine was doing, too, even if she didn't know it, when she promised to bring me with her. In order to protect them, we tell all kinds of lies to the people we love.

TODAY IS THE EIGHTH DAY OF MANMAN'S prayers, and tomorrow we will liberate her soul from captivity under the sea.

I'm at the cove with Mackenson, where the sea is calm and flat. In the distance, a man in a dugout canoe tosses his fishing net into the water. The sunlight glints off the rolling waves like shining silver. Mackenson peels off his T-shirt and pants until he is wearing a ragged pair of basketball shorts. Shirtless, he doesn't look like a boy at all. All those days of walking up mountains, climbing trees, and wielding hoes and pickaxes have given him the body of a man. His arms are muscular and contoured; his torso is narrow but powerful.

I look away when I realize I'm staring at him.

"Just get into the water," Mackenson says. "It's not deep."

"I don't know how to swim. I didn't grow up diving for conch and making fishing nets like you did."

"It's really easy. And you'll float without trying. Just float and kick your feet, and you'll be fine."

I slip out of my blouse and jeans and fold them and place them on a piece of driftwood. I'm wearing an orange bikini that used to be Nadine's, which is too big for me now. By the time my toes touch the water, Mackenson is already way out in the surf, diving and surfacing like a fish. The low, gentle waves rush up and over my feet, leaving trails of white foam. "Come on, Magdalie!" he calls. "Just kick your feet!"

"Uh-uh. Never!" I yell back. "Swimming is so natural to you, you don't even know how to teach it." I lower myself into the shallow water near the shore, where I can sit and the water comes up no higher than my waist. It is sun-warm and sky blue. I lie back. I didn't bring a shower cap. My hair will get salty, and I'll have to wash it. It doesn't matter. *You'll float without trying.* Slowly I let myself drift away from shore. Water fills my ears, and all I can hear is the deep inhale-exhale of the tide. The sea is salty, and my body feels weightless in it. Mackenson is right: I float.

Did Manman ever swim here as a child? I close my eyes to the bright sun, and the sounds of the sea sing to me. *Was she ever held and rocked by these waves?*

I float. The water is so warm and lulling. The sun is hot, like a hand on my face. I imagine my body slipping away. I don't know how long I float, so long I stop caring whether I float or sink. And I imagine: *Lasirèn, the mermaid spirit of the sea, comes and takes my hand. She pulls me away, under the water. My hair streams out behind me. It is a beautiful place, full of wonders. She takes me under the water, anba dlo, to where the lwa and the ancestors are, where all dead souls go, to where Manman waits for me.*

A hand grips my arm. It's Mackenson. "Magdalie!" he shouts. I try to stand up, but I'm too far out, farther out than I ever thought I would go. My feet can't find the bottom, and the water around my legs is dark and cold. There might be sharks down there. There might be mermaids down there. My head slips under, and I cough on salt water. Mackenson keeps hold of my arm and pulls me back toward shore.

"I didn't think you'd go out that far!" he exclaims.

The water grows shallow and warm again. Mackenson looks worried, the water slick on his skin, sparkling in his hair.

"I thought I'd lost you," he says. "Where were you, Magda? Where were you?"

"I'm swimming to escape, brother, I'm swimming to escape." I laugh and laugh. Our presidents have been telling us this for years: *naje pou sòti!* They've been telling Haitian people to just keep trying, keep struggling, and someday we'll be free. "If I just swim hard enough, I can get anywhere, monchè!"

Mackenson doesn't laugh. He stares at me, his eyes wide and filled with wonder, and looks a little scared.

THERE ARE NO CEMETERIES HERE. INSTEAD, the dead remain among us. Many houses have tombs in the lakou, amid the banana stalks, the thorns, the guava trees. The tombs are small, for perhaps four people, and made of mud, brightly painted in shades of white, sea-green, bright blue, and pink, all covered in thatched canopies to keep the worst of the rain away. When you walk from Tonton Benisoit's house to Mme Frantz's lakou, you pass right by a pink tomb nestled in the trees, not far from where the boys play soccer barefoot in the scrubby grass, where the palm fronds trace shadows on the red earth.

Manman was buried in the empty space in the tomb beside Matant Jezila's house, down by the sea. You can hear the waves from there. It is a pretty blue-and-white tomb, clean, with a chunky white cross on top of it.

There is only peace here. So far from Port-au-Prince, from the crush and the noise, the filth and the dust. This is a place where grief blows lightly.

"Who else is buried there?" I ask Matant Marie-Lourdes.

"Madanm Sento is there," she replies. "They say she was a hundred and twenty when she died." She begins to laugh. "She was the strictest, meanest old lady in all of Saint Juste, with long, long white hair. She was bent over like an old wire hanger, and she used to curse at all the kids who'd come knocking mangoes out of her tree."

"And who else?"

"Benita's nephew Wilmer. He was only three years old. He got malaria in his brain and he died before they could get him down the mountain to the clinic."

"Oh! Poor little boy."

"You see, Magdalie, life isn't sweet here," says Matant Marie-Lourdes quietly. "We are healthy only until we get sick, and when we get sick, there is nowhere to go. We don't need money to live, until we need money not to die." There's no anger in her voice as she says this. These are simple facts, clear as the sky above.

The last day of the denyè priyè is a party. It's a good-bye party for Tonton Élie, Michlove, and me, too, because we have to go back to Port-au-Prince soon. "We did what we came to do." Tonton Élie nods. "There's nothing left for us here."

"Yeah," I say, but I think: *Nothing doesn't mean no one.*

"I know things haven't been easy for you, Magdalie,"

Tonton Élie adds haltingly. He can't look me in the eye. It's funny and awkward to watch him try to be nice, because his kindness is usually guarded in thorns.

"It's okay, Uncle," I interrupt. "You don't have to say it."

"I'm just saying—let's try to make things different. I'll try to make things different."

To prepare for the party, all the women of St. Juste came to Matant Marie-Lourdes's kitchen this morning, where they sit on their heels or on low straw chairs, peeling, chopping, pounding, and chatting all day. Billows of delicious-smelling smoke emanate from the open walls of the kitchen, stretching high into the clear blue sky.

Joanne and I spend the afternoon doing each other's hair and makeup. I brought lip gloss and sparkly black eyeliner from Port-au-Prince, and she's got a compact with a rainbow of eye shadow. "I want every color!" she declares.

"You'll look like a prostitute," mutters Matant Marie-Lourdes.

I straighten Joanne's hair with a curling iron, heated up in the charcoal. She fusses and teases little Béa for the coarseness of her hair. "Look at this tèt grenn," she mutters. "What can I do with this?"

"You're as much of a tèt grenn as she is," I remind her.

I braid Joanne's hair into ti kouri—some start at the nape of her neck and go up, and others start at her forehead and go back, and they gather together into a ponytail on top. She looks like Rihanna. I've got a bounda poul bun, high on my head—with a piece of a kerchief stuffed inside the hair, so it's flat and round like a chicken butt—with a green ribbon tied around it.

"You look like a princess." Joanne giggles. "Let's see what your boyfriend says. He's going to say, 'Oh, how pretty, my cheri!'"

My heart jumps. "What boyfriend? I don't have a boyfriend!"

"Oh! *You* know."

I feel myself blushing, because I know they are right: I've been dressing up all day for Mackenson.

Tonton Élie has set up huge speakers in front of the house, running off an old Delco, blaring konpa that people can hear all the way up and down the mountain. While it is still light out, little children begin to dance, imitating grown-ups, moving their hips and kicking out their feet.

This is the last day we are allowed to cry for Manman. This is the end of mourning, and it marks the moment when we are supposed to move on. We have liberated her spirit from where it dwelled in the cold underwater. We have released her from this mortal life. After this, if I want to cry, I will do it secretly, so that people will not get angry with me. I feel sad, thinking of this. Not because Manman is gone—that's a different sadness. Now I am sad because her death isn't new anymore, and because the world and my life have continued to turn without her. There was a comfort when the wound was fresh, because it meant that Manman was here—that she existed, that she was important, that she was part of our everyday life. Now we have not only buried her, but we've buried the loss itself.

A huge round moon has risen, butter-yellow and glowing. I'm standing on the porch, leaning against a corner of the house and staring up at heaven, when Mackenson comes up to me, takes my hand, and asks me to dance. The song is *"Pa leve men'w sou li,"* which I used to hear all the time in Port-au-Prince, in taptaps. It's a catchy, swirling melody, cheerful and bittersweet at once.

"Okay," I say.

He's a good dancer. He holds me tightly against him, as people do dancing konpa, and we move in unison. I feel warm and sweet. He brushes a lock of hair from my face.

I feel happy, light, and relaxed from the kleren; my lips tingle. The world seems strange and new tonight. Everything feels possible and okay. Everything is okay, for this moment. The black, starry sky is shallow, as though the air around me were no deeper than the depth of a needle held in my outstretched hand, as though I could reach out and graze that yellow moon with my fingertips. Everything is peace, and there is no world beyond this corner of a mountain, beyond this swirling sweet konpa, beyond the soft weight of Mackenson pressed against me, his hand on my back, guiding me. The music is happy; the laughter is happy. Everything feels ecstatic and desperate. Blurrily, I think of sex, and

I think of death. I realize: Every moment of joyous celebration contains the seed of death.

"Je t'aime, I love you," whispers Mackenson, so softly that I almost think I've imagined it.

I don't say anything. I don't want to hurt him, but I also cannot lie. I just squeeze his hand. Maybe, someday, I might be able to love him back. But right now, I can't see him the same way he sees me, and I look into his kind and trusting face, and I wish I could accept simple love. But I don't have space for simple love in my heart or my head, at least not yet. It would have to fight with anger and fear and sadness, and, some days, anger, fear, and sadness are still winning.

"I know," I murmur. "I know."

"WOULD YOU STAY IF YOU COULD?" ASKS Mackenson. We are sitting side by side on the huge exposed roots of Tonton Seneren's mango tree, which are almost as high and wide as church pews. It is my last afternoon here. I hate good-byes. Since Nadou left, every good-bye feels like forever.

I know Mackenson is really asking, "Would you stay here with me if you could, if I asked you to?" But I cannot go down that path, and I cannot allow him to go down it, either. So I laugh and say as lightly as I can, "I'll miss not having an avocado tree right in front of my house in Port-au-Prince. That's the best thing here!"

His voice is quiet. "Oh! You're clever . . ." He knows how to hear what I am not brave enough to say.

The earth is for cultivating and for burying. I hadn't liked to think of Manman lying in the dust of Port-au-

Prince, amid the rubble and the garbage, in the ground and the city that had killed her. I feel a little more peaceful now, knowing that her bones are here, in the tomb with her ancestors, in the soil her family had cultivated, that had nourished her during her childhood, in the ground she had once perhaps played hopscotch or oslè upon, years ago, as a little girl.

I imagine all of us, everyone who loved Manman. Me and Nadine. Tonton Élie. Tonton Benisoit and Matant Marie-Lourdes. All her brothers and sisters who are still alive, and their children, my cousins. The machann she used to buy vegetables from every day, who would sometimes give her a hot cup of sweet coffee and invite her to sit and rest. The old man selling bread who always gave her an extra piece. We link hands and form a huge net, and we carry her—we carry Manman, her bones and her dreams, back to her home. And then, at last, we give her up to the ones we cannot see. We give her to the ancestors, to her own manman and papa, to her dead brothers, to the spirits. *Welcome,* they say, and they embrace her, and she goes to join them.

"I'm scared," I tell Mackenson, looking out, one last time, over the sea. "I don't know if I belong in Port-au-Prince anymore. I don't want to think about the earthquake anymore."

Mackenson doesn't tell me not to be scared. He just says, "We'll always wait for you here." And then he asks, "What will you do there?"

"I'll go to school," I say. "I don't know how I'll do it, but I will."

I am filled with hope and fear, because I want so much for my future, and I don't know how I will do it, but I know I must do it.

When at last it is time to go, a parade of people walk us to Abricots, single file in the early summer sun, down the red path filled with roots and thorned bushes, snaking down the mountain. Tonton Élie carries a sack of breadfruit. Michlove carries baby Yolène. Mackenson carries my suitcase. Matant Marie-Lourdes carries a plastic bowl of boiled yams and sauce, tied up in a black plastic bag, for me to eat on the long trip. Joanne carries a basketful of sweet kenèp. Tonton Benisoit carries a heavy sack on his back, an old Tchako rice bag filled with coconuts, plantains, yams, pineapples, and avocados from his garden.

When we finally get to Abricots, we refresh ourselves in the cool, sweet water of the lagoon, where all around us women scrub laundry and children splash, playing and bathing. Life marches on, no matter who is a part of it and who has left it. And now it is time to get on the motorcycle taxi to Jérémie.

Tonton Élie settles Michlove and the baby in the center of the moto, then gets on the back, balancing a suitcase on his head with one hand. As my waiting moto driver ties the sack of breadfruit to the back and wipes the dust off his machine, I hug and kiss everyone good-bye.

"When will you come back?" asks Joanne.

"I don't know."

"Will you forget us?" asks Joanne. "Will you let us go?"

"No," I reply. "No, no."

"I don't believe you," she says, and she shrugs.

Tonton Benisoit sets down his sack. "Take care of yourself, pitit mwen. *Pòte w byen.*"

Something in his words makes my eyes prickle. I am in perpetual motion. Another departure, another ending, another good-bye. *Good-bye. I wish I could stay, but the place that I dread is also the only place of promise.*

When Mackenson and I embrace, no longer and no shorter than I've hugged anyone else, I slip a folded-up piece of paper into his hand.

Mackenson asks, "When will I see you again, Magdalie?"

My smile feels sad. It's a different smile from the one I used to have, as if it's an older person's smile, worn and heavy with experience and containing the distance of the world.

Down the cracked red-earth footpaths through banana leaves and thorns, down to the place where the sea waves meet sweet, fresh water, where children splash and fishermen in wide straw hats take to the sea in handmade sailboats and haul in their catch—that is where I have traveled. And over the sea and past the horizon, onto the capital, and to that other world—that is where I am returning. Later, Mackenson will open the page I've left in his hand, after I have already grown smaller and smaller, riding the back of the moto-taxi down Abricots's paved streets, disappearing up and over the dusty mountain to Jérémie, and onto the boat that will carry me out of his life, for now, at least, to Port-au-Prince through the night.

Home is etched into my memory and my bones.
Home is
Port-au-Prince
city of haze, city of my youth,
city of crumbled gray concrete, city of rebar,
city of noise,
city of konpa, bachata, and rap blasting from storefronts,
city of merchants, city of tarps
city of camps, city of victims
city of corpses
city-turned-graveyard
city of survivors
city of sewage, city of thieves,
city of garbage, city of churches, city of schools
city of children
city of taptaps painted with soccer stars and Bible verses;
city of promise, city of loss,
city of lost hope.
Home is
Jérémie
land of my mother
land where my ancestors are buried
land of the mountain, land of the sea,
land of avocados as large as my head
land of coral-rock, land of long-beaked birds

land of no-more-possibility
land without high school, land without hospital
land without a future,
land of my escape, land of my recovery,
land of my first love.
Home is
the ocean wide and deep
sea of spirits, passage of ancestors,
sea of imagination, passage of myth,
sea of blackness, passage of our theft,
sea of rape, passage of humiliation,
sea of transformation
where we became slaves
sea of what was lost
and what remains.
Home is
in me
Home is
always with me
Home is
inscribed in my heart, my mind
my flesh, my bones,
Like the cement dust that blows out over the bay
And sinks, and settles, and sediments at the bottom of the sea.

OCTOBER 2011

SOMETIMES THINGS FEEL OKAY NOW.

Michlove and baby Yolène moved to the capital with us, finally. Tonton Élie is sending Michlove to a free program at a Protestant church, where she is learning to read and write. I do love Yolène, who has four teeth, and who is so smart that she has learned to grin and announce *"Pipi! Pipi!"* whenever she wets herself. Élie picks up free condoms sometimes and blows them up like balloons for Yolène. Michlove still isn't very interesting, but sometimes it's nice to have other people around.

Last week I went to see Safira and her little boy. I didn't tell Tonton Élie I was going into the middle of Cité Soleil, because he always talks bad about "those people" and how they're criminals. I guess no matter how poor you are, you always need to feel better than somebody.

"*Chouchouuuuuu!*" Safira shouted when she saw me, and she hugged me so tightly that she almost knocked me over. "Magdalie! Child! How *are* you? I'm so glad to see you! Come in and meet my manman!"

Theirs is a neat little concrete house surrounded by rubble. "It's not from the earthquake," Safira told me matter-of-factly when she saw me looking. "It's from the years of war, when MINUSTAH soldiers were looking for the bandi, and there was shooting all the time." The broken lots are filled with rainwater and blackish mud, where garbage and clumps of feathery green algae have collected, and mosquitoes breed along the top. Ducks wade in and nibble at things. We had to play hopscotch to get to the front door.

"You are Magdalie!" exclaimed Safira's mother, embracing me. "Cheri, I have heard so much about you! I'm sorry about our little house. You see we have the sea right outside." She laughed and gestured to the flat expanses of trash-filled rainwater beyond their front door.

"It's okay, it's okay," I said. "You don't have to be ashamed of anything." The house smelled like bleach and sheets dried in the sun. Safira's manman looked so much like Safira. She was thin, but she didn't look dried-out and old like someone with TB.

"Are you well now?" I asked her.

"Oh, yes, yes," she said. "Those medications weren't easy, no! But I'm not coughing anymore. They wouldn't let me have the baby here if I was coughing. Will you drink some coffee? We don't have any food right now, just coffee and bread. Will you have coffee, pitit?"

"Manman!" exclaimed Safira, embarrassed and pleased at the same time. "Come see Edensky, Magda," she murmured excitedly. "He's sleeping."

She took my hand and pulled me into the other room, where the baby was sleeping on his back in the middle of the bed. He made soft sounds. His hair was black and silky. Safira gently got onto the bed and curled her body around him and began fanning her hand back and forth, keeping the mosquitoes away.

"He already had malaria once," she whispered.

If only the power of her love were enough to ensure his future. What a terrifying love. Safira must know every second contains the possibility of losing her entire world.

I examined little Edensky's plump, sleeping face, sticky with sweat, and tried hard to imagine him growing up: in his first school uniform, running through the Cité, chubby knees bobbing up and down.

"I'll take care of him, I promise," said Safira, as though she knew what was in my mind. "He's going to have a good life."

There will always be children. There will be children whose parents work in other people's houses or cross the border to cut cane, whose fathers take a boat to search for life, whose mothers work the streets selling food or clothes or vegetables or their bodies. There will always be children whose parents love them so much, they'd give them away and let them go. In a just world, love could keep them all from sinking.

"I'll go hungry so he can eat if I need to. I will. And

I'll send him to preschool, and by the time he's older, primary school will be free . . ."

His tiny pink hand gripped her finger as he slept, and she studied it with such fierce intimacy that I knew she was making a covenant. *Here's all I can promise you: that I'll try to be the hero of your one small life.*

Safira's mother came in and gave me a tin cup of coffee and a packet of Guarina crackers. "Next time you come, I'll cook you a real meal. Do you eat salami?"

"When are you coming back?" asked Safira. "When will I see you again?"

"Soon."

"Don't lie."

"No, I will. I will."

"And you'll come to his baptism."

"Yes, I'll come."

"Okay. I believe you." And Safira bent over her baby boy and began, quietly, to sing.

Dodo, do ti pitit manman,
Si ou pa dodo,
dyab la va manje w,
Dodo dodo ti pitit manman,
Dyab la va manje w.

Sleep, mama's little one.
If you don't sleep,
The devil will eat you.
Sleep, mama's little one
Sleep, the devil will eat you.

WE ARE PREPARING TO LEAVE THE CAMP behind. They say that soon—though we don't know if it's weeks or months—an NGO is going to come and give every tent $500 US and then break the tents down with hammers. Every day now Tonton Élie goes out looking for a room we can rent. It will work out okay for us. I refuse to think it won't work out for us.

We got a kitten to catch rats and cockroaches. He is brown and gray with the stripes of a miniature tiger. Tonton Élie said we'd just call him Mimi, but I said no, we had to give him a real name, so I'm calling him Kirikou after the cartoon, because he is small but brave. I say, "*Kiri-kiri-kiri-kou!*" He says, "*Miaou*" with his bright pink tongue. He sleeps in my bed with me, curled up against my chest.

I hear from Nadine sometimes. I go to the Internet

café, when I have some money, and log on to Facebook. Nadou posts photos of herself, in Miami, standing on the beach with people I don't know.

She'll write, Ki jan ou ye, bou? How r u? on my wall.

And I'll write back, I'm fine, chouchou, wi. I'm not bad. It's easier over Facebook, close yet distant, nothing like a phone call at all.

Nadine is present and not present. She is connected to my life, but it is not the same thing at all. I know, now, not to ask her about anything else—not to ask her when she will send for me, when she will get my visa. I turn off my heart and pretend that I haven't waited all these months for her to mention it to me.

I WAS HEADING DOWN ROUTE DELMAS LATE this morning, trying to get to Wharf Jérémie to pick up some white yams and salt fish that Tonton Benisoit was sending with my cousin Jonas on the boat.

I was trying to flag down a taptap to Kalfou Avyasyon when a car stopped behind me and I heard someone call, "Magdalie!" The voice was instantly familiar, but the person's name wouldn't coalesce in my mind. "Magda-*lie*!" I turned around.

Mme Faustin had gotten out of the car. A sudden apparition. Her eyes popped and burned like a demon's. "Oh-oh, Magdalie. You're ignoring me like a dog in the street?"

I wanted to escape and couldn't. I wanted to be anywhere else in the world than right there, in front of Mme Faustin. Her voice was huge, her presence was huge, her chest jutted like a general's. I stood gasping and gaping like a dying fish flopping around in the bottom of a canoe.

"Bonjour, madame," I said. My stomach hurt.

"Are you in school?"

"No."

"Where is your sister?"

"In Miami."

"You never come see me. Ungrateful child." Her lips pursed into a sour, fleshy frown, and I thought she might strike me. "You never come see me. After all I ever did for you people." Her eyes shone with true pain. I think: *Crybaby.*

But I don't say anything. What we always learned—what Manman taught us, without ever telling us in words—was to keep your mouth shut and your head down. That's how it has to be, when you're the servant's family and they can send you away whenever they want, when they can take away everything, when your home and your life and even your body were never really your own in the first place.

You're free, Magdalie, I told myself. *Magdalie, aren't you free?*

I made my voice perfectly calm and smooth, like boiled milk that's been run through a strainer. "You're wrong, Madame Faustin."

I was standing there alone on the sidewalk, facing her, but I was not alone. I clenched my hot fist, and I visualized everyone I've ever loved, alive and dead, holding hands and sending strength and patience to me.

They formed an invisible chain of souls and became the stuff of protection and God.

"You are wrong. We're the ones who lost someone. You were supposed to come see *us*. You were supposed to come to our house and see us. That's how it works."

Mme Faustin's face quivered, in anger or despair. "I miss her," Mme Faustin whispered, her eyes shimmering like melting ice. "I *miss* her."

"Then why didn't you treat her better? Why did you keep her on her feet all day, even when she was sick? Why did you call her to your room at all hours of the night, for whatever little tiny nothing reason? Why did you never pay her enough to have a better life than she had? Why did you say she was your family, but you made her walk behind you, carrying your handbag in church like she was your slave?"

I didn't feel angry as I said any of this. I'd stopped feeling it. I could have been reciting multiplication tables. I don't have anything to prove, and I'm as bare as bones.

Bruised fury flashed through her eyes. "Yolette was my family. I always took care of her. I always took care of you and your sister. I lost my home that day, too. I lost everything I had. Magdalie, why do you hate me so much?"

Mme Faustin didn't look so much like a general now. She looked old and sad, older than she did two years ago, as if her flesh had pulled away from the inside of her skin.

"No. I'm the one who lost everything I had." But even

as I said it, I knew it wasn't really true. For a long time I thought I had; I thought I'd lost everything. I saw my dreams stripped away, one by one, peeled off and tossed into the gutter like the petals off a dead flower. I will never go to America. I will never see Nadine again. I will never go back to school. But I've still got Tonton Élie and everyone in St. Juste. I have Mackenson, and I have Safira, too. I've got my memories, which I float on and through all day. I've still got Manman and Nadou as they live in my mind: the ghosts I love. And I've still got myself.

"Why do you hate me so much, Magdalie?" asked Mme Faustin again. "After all I've done for you, why do you hate me?"

"I don't hate you, Madame. I just don't want to see you."

And I walked away. I had nothing more to say. I jumped on the next taptap for Kalfou Avyasyon, squeezed in next to an old man and a woman with a baby, and rode it all the way down Delmas. Past the Dominican beauty salons and the cracked old Sogebank building, through this breathing, shifting city. I rode down to Avyasyon and got off the taptap, slipping through the crowds, making my way to the wharf. I was invisible, another anonymous shadow on the street.

Wharf Jérémie is always mayhem when the boats come in, sea-green and creaking. These ferries! Back and forth they go, from Jérémie to Port-au-Prince. They are dangerous, but they are our lifeblood.

A hot, pressing swirl of people jostled forward to unload, sell, bargain, receive. If I could find the right kind of coconut, I'd buy one for Michlove as a peace offering. But my first priority was finding Jonas and picking up the yams and fish. A big salted sunfish. There will always be these small moments of pleasure. Small, good things. I should content myself with them and stop asking God for too much.

I get home late in the afternoon, arms aching but pretty pleased with myself. My plastic woven sack bulges with big yams and some big green plantains and not one but two salted fish (a dorad and a jofi, which I love because it's just got one big long bone you can pull out all at once). I'm happy because we have food, and because if Tonton Benisoit has enough yams and salted fish to send this much to us, he must be having an okay season—the rains enough but not too much. And there is something else, too: a bunch of juicy kenèp, picked by Mackenson from his tree and sent to Port-au-Prince just for me.

Tonton Élie is half working, half watching a soccer game with the volume on low, Chelsea versus somebody, when I return. Not Real Madrid or the volume would be super high. It's background noise as he pries the back off an old radio and starts prodding around inside.

I sit down and wipe the sweat from my brow with my handkerchief. I always feel filthy when I get home, covered in dust and sweat, but it's not good to bathe with cold water when you're already hot. Tonton Élie cracks his knuckles expectantly. "I have good news for you, Magdalie."

"Yeah? What have you got for me, uncle-of-mine?" I pick up Yolène and bounce her in my arms. She squeals with delight, wrinkling her little nose and showing her four tiny teeth. She reaches out a hand, and I clamp it between my lips and pretend to bite it.

He wordlessly reaches into his jeans pocket, draws out an envelope, and hands it to me. I take it, confused, and hold it in my cupped hands as if I don't know what it is or what to do with it.

"Well, open it, Magda."

"What is it?" The small package feels heavy, solid and compact, a little soft. I know exactly what it feels like. But I don't want to begin to hope that it's what it feels like.

I open it. And it's what I think it is.

It's a wad of money. Twenty-five 1,000-gourde bills, rolled up and bound with an orange rubber band. I've never held this much money in my life. I don't think very many Haitians have.

"It's money for you to go to school," says Tonton Élie. "Magdalie, you will go to school."

"Oh, no, Tonton," I say. This money could buy food for us for months. Enough rice to fill the bedroom. Milk for Yolène. Cooking oil. Dried beans. Charcoal. Medicine. Or . . . I could go buy cosmetics at the Dominican border and sell them for a profit. We could do so many different things with this money. "I couldn't. Oh, let's buy food with it instead."

"It was given to you on the condition that you use it to go to school."

I narrow my eyes at Tonton Élie. There's something suspicious in his tone and his face. It's the same strange, evasive expression he got when he told me about the flowers on the place Manman was buried behind Mme Faustin's house—

"Ohhh . . ." My breath comes out in a punctured sigh. "Oh, Madame Faustin."

Tonton Élie nods and shrugs. "She stopped by when you were down at the wharf."

"But, Tonton, there's so much we could do with this much money."

"Magdalie." Now his tone is severe. "You are still a child. You belong in school."

I am not a child anymore. Still, images begin to flood my mind before I can stop myself—all my old, dead dreams, reanimated. I see myself ironing my uniform, walking to school, getting my black shoes shined. I see myself studying chemistry and French. I see myself in a few years, taking the rhéto and philo exams. All these things I had stopped daring to dream about. Now I know for certain I am not the girl I once was. A year ago, I could think only of Miami, of Nadine, of escaping the world I knew. Sometimes it's easier to have a dream that remains ungraspable, just out of reach. But maybe those dreams stop you from living in the world right in front of your eyes.

But why? Why is Mme Faustin doing this?

Is she giving me the money because she loved Manman—or even because she loves me? Or is she doing it because doing this one good thing for me allows her to love herself? I remember her face as I last saw it, older, brimming with worry and sorrow. Pity engraved into the lines between her eyebrows, the lines at the corners of her mouth. Does she feel sorry for me or sorry for herself? Is she doing this because it is the right thing to do, or because she wants to absolve herself for Manman's death and how she treated her all those years?

And maybe it doesn't matter. Hate the dog, but admit its teeth are white. She is sad, and mean-hearted, and alone, and for a moment, I pity her enough to forgive her and to set myself free. Next month, I will be back in school. I will be back on the path to the future. *Be thankful, Magdalie,* I tell myself. *Let go. Be happy. Let yourself be happy.*

It seems that a lot of people want me to believe in fairness and morality. That's what we hear in church, that if you follow the rules and accept your lot, and if you do right by others rather than follow your own pleasure, you'll be rewarded (in the next life, if not in this one). It's what we hear on the silly public-service announcements that the government puts on the TV and radio: Ti Joel washes his hands, and he doesn't get cholera; smart, aware people build their houses out of good materials, and they don't die in earthquakes. It's what the soap operas show—whatever happens in the middle, the villains never win. It seems everyone is telling me that if you just make enough of an effort, you'll deserve and find a happy ending.

I don't suppose I've ever really believed it works that way. It feels as if life is just like playing the lotto against someone who's rigged the game. But we keep playing anyway—pooling our coins every week in hope of an eventual payout, even though we know the system is against us.

I don't need a miracle; I don't need a swimming pool or a lot of power or money. I don't need a new car or a Whirlpool washing machine. I don't need to be better than anyone else. I just need a chance to gather up my wishes, to write my own ending, in which everything is the way it's supposed to be.

JANUARY 2020

An Ending, by Magdalie Jean-Baptiste

TWO YOUNG WOMEN STAND AND LOOK AT their reflection in the mirror. Nadine leans close and makes her eyes wide to put on mascara (she's always been afraid of poking herself in the eye), and Magdalie stands farther back, applying lip gloss with her little finger. They are surprised to see how much they still look alike after all these years. Magdalie had imagined that Nadine would have grown as fat as an American missionary. But there they are, still: same soft, dark skin, same eyes, same gap between their teeth. They can still wear each other's clothes.

"What was the best thing about Miami?" Magdalie asks.

Nadine thinks for a moment. "There wasn't very much trash on the streets," she says. "And there wasn't chaos or unrest. There were drive-through hamburger restaurants. But I always missed Haiti. Haiti is my home." She wipes away a few specks of black mascara that have smudged under her eye. "And I missed my family."

"What was the worst thing?"

"Too many Haitians," Nadine says immediately, then laughs. "No. That's a joke. The worst thing was feeling poor. Because in Haiti, so many people are poor, it's nothing to be ashamed of. And there's always a way to degaje*, to get by, even when you have nothing. But misery in the United States is harder than misery in Haiti. You feel like it's your fault for being poor. And if you don't have any money, you can't eat. You won't have a house. If you fall, there's nowhere to go and no one to catch you. Everyone back in Haiti assumes that once you've arrived* lòt bò*, that it's a good life, that you're living well. And it feels so shameful to tell anyone that it's not true."*

"Have you come back to Haiti for good?"

"Yes. I'll stay here. You know, I was just there to get my nursing degree and come back. I'll work here."

"Nurse Nadine." Magdalie smiles. "I thought you would never come back. I thought you had abandoned us forever."

Nadine looks at Magdalie, her eyes shining. "Sista," she says, "I can't lie to you. There were times I didn't call for months. I couldn't bring myself to do it. Hearing your voice hurt too much. I felt as though I couldn't do enough for you. I missed you so much, and it felt worse to only have a little bit of you and not have the real thing. Sometimes I'd pretend in my head that I was a different person, someone who didn't have ties to anyone in the world. Like I was an actress in a movie. It was easier."

"I missed you every day," says Magdalie quietly. "Sometimes I hated you."

"Have you ever loved anyone so much you couldn't stand it?" Nadine asks. "That's what it was like."

The country has changed. Magdalie had never dared to hope for so much. Now she looks at the road and thinks: I hardly recognize it, it is so clean. Where garbage and sewage and cloudy, charcoal-stained water once flowed, there are now low, eager saplings.

The public plazas and parks are green once again, filled with children playing and young couples kissing. Vendors sell cold soft drinks and ice cream bars out of clean, modern carts, and old people with canes take slow afternoon strolls. The air is dustless and clear.

The Haitian state demanded reparations from France and, at last, received them. They demanded damages from the United States and the international community and, at last, received them. Most of the old rubble was hauled into distant mountains or dropped into the sea, but some of it was saved. In various places throughout the city—downtown, on the Champ de Mars, on Place Boyer, on every university and school campus, in the courtyards of hospitals and churches—are monuments to the earthquake victims, constructed by Haitian artists from the broken cement and twisted metal wreckage. And out in the hills to the north of the capital, where the dead were buried by the tens of thousands, is a museum commemorating the quake. A stone wall has engraved upon it all the names that could be found (Nadine and Magdalie's manman's name is among them). There are photos of before and after, and photos of the dead before they were dead (when they were smiling or serious, but, in whatever case, when they were alive). Photos, shot from above, of the camps, spreading like patchwork seas. And there are displays, too—a child's school desk, broken when the roof fell. A pair of tattered, dusty leather shoes. A pair of women's jeans, ripped and covered in long-dried blood. Drawings by children who once lived in camps. And everyone is forced to remember, and no one will ever forget, and the dead at last will forgive.

Now there are no more camps. All the people who lived in them have had the choice of whether to stay in the capital (where new, anti-seismic housing projects were built out in La Plaine and in some of the places where the camps used to be) or move to the provinces. And many people chose to leave Port-au-Prince, because now there are good secondary schools and hospitals everywhere, in all the ten departments of Haiti, and because the state started a huge reforestation campaign and then made a law that gave people subsidies to buy Haitian rice and Haitian vegetables. They built a system of railroads to bring produce from the countryside to the cities—not only Port-au-Prince but to the other cities, too. When Haitian products became cheaper than Dominican and American ones, farmers started to make a living, and everyone was happy, because they could afford to buy Haitian rice all the time. And once people started leaving the capital and going to the provinces, the congested, teeming urban quarters started to thin out and become livable neighborhoods again, and people didn't have to live ten to a room, the houses all on top of one another, anymore.

All the buildings in the country are earthquake-proof now, just like in Japan. No one is afraid to be under a concrete roof anymore. People don't have to jump whenever a truck rumbles by anymore. People don't have to sleep with one eye open anymore.

Once people started to become happy and hopeful again, they started to believe that change could keep happening. And because they believed, they started to be able to put their heads together again to make sound plans. And they found honest leaders, because finally they knew that things could get better and that the future didn't have to contain only hopelessness, lies, and corruption.

Tonton Élie got a loan to set up his own small electronics shop on Lalue. And Safira's family made enough money farming rice and lalo out in the Artibonite that they sent Edensky to a good Catholic school in St. Marc. And little Yolène grew from a baby into a little girl in Port-au-Prince, and she was never very sick, and when she did get sick, it was never a problem to take her to the doctor. And Mackenson was right, he was right all along: he stayed in Jérémie and became an agronomist—he got an education and kept working the land.

In the end, they all were saved, everyone Magdalie had known, everyone she had ever worried about. They were saved; they were delivered.

And the bones of the unknown dead—the nameless slaves killed in passage and in captivity, the unremembered victims of dictatorships and coups, the never-found earthquake dead buried in the ruins of the old city—ceased to be ground to dust beneath their feet.

Who knew that Port-au-Prince could be so beautiful? When they were children, Magdalie and Nadine had only seen it that way in history books, frozen images in sepia or black-and-white. Now, living and breathing, it glistens like a pearl in the sun.

Two sisters, so different and so alike, separated for so long but never more than a soul's width apart. The sun sets over the gleaming, reborn city and blinks nearly green as it drops below the sparkling bay, and the sisters set off down the dustless road together, arm in arm, into the future, as they speak, in hushed voices, about everything good that has ever happened in their lives.

• · • · • · • · •

Glossary

A general note on Haitian Creole pronunciation: Haitian Creole (Kreyòl) is a phonetic language. With a few guidelines, it's easy to learn how to pronounce. The **r** is something like a French guttural "r," pronounced in the back of the throat, though sometimes in Creole the **r** sound becomes more like an English "w" sound. **Ch** sounds like the English "sh." **J** sounds like a French "j," while **dj** sounds more like an English "j." The vowels **a**, **e**, **i**, and **o** are long vowels. **Ou** sounds like the English "oo." **Ay** makes the sound of English "eye." **An**, **en**, **on**, and **oun** are nasal vowels: the "n" is not pronounced but rather denotes that the vowel should be pronounced in the nose. Vowels with accents (è and ò) are more open than the accentless versions of those vowels.

Ala traka (AH-la TRAH-ka) — "What a problem!"

Anmwèy (ahnm-WAY) — an exclamation or interjection, literally meaning "Help me!" but often used jokingly or in exaggerated fashion

asòsi (ah-soh-SEE) — a bitter leaf, often boiled into a tea and used to treat fevers and other illnesses

banann bouyi (bah-NAHN bou-YEE) — boiled plantains

Bay piti pa chich (bye pee-TEE pah SHEESH) — "To give just a little isn't stingy."

bidonville (French) (bee-don-VEEL) — poor, overcrowded urban neighborhood *boubou* (boo-boo) — a term of endearment

bounda (boon-DAH) — bottom, booty, butt

cheri (shay-REE) — a term of endearment

chouchou (shoo-shoo) — a term of endearment

chouchoun (shoo-SHOON) — a sweet, motherly way of referring to female genitalia

degaje (deh-gah-ZHAY) — to get by, to manage somehow

djolè (joh-LEH) — a big-mouth, a show-off

dlo (dlo) — water

doudou (doo-doo) — a term of endearment

dous makòs (DOOS mah-KOHS) — a kind of candy, similar to a stiff caramel or *dulce de leche*, with distinctive beige and pink stripes

Ezili Dantò (EH-zee-lee dahn-TOH) — One incarnation of the spirit Ezili. Ezili Dantò is a dark-skinned woman with scars on her face who holds a child. She can be both vengeful and protective.

fritay (free-TIE) — fried snacks, often sold as street food

Gede (geh-deh) — the often raucous spirit of the underworld

gòl (gohl) — a long stick used to knock fruit out of trees *goudougoudou* (goo-DOO-goo-DOO) — the sound of the earthquake; one way to refer to the earthquake

Jezi (jheh-ZEE) — Jesus

kamyonèt (kahm-yo-NEHT) — a pick-up truck, often elaborately painted, used as public transport

kenèp (keh-NEHP) — a small green fruit resembling a lime, with sweet-sour pink-orange flesh (*quenepa* or *limoncillo* in Spanish)

Kirikou (kee-ree-KOO) — French animated film, based on West African folktales, which has considerable international distribution, including regular broadcasts on Haitian television. It concerns a tiny, brave little boy named Kirikou who rescues his village from a sorceress.

kivèt (kee-VEHT) — a metal or plastic basin in which to bathe, do laundry, etc.

kleren (kleh-REN) — undistilled homemade sugar cane liquor

kokòt (ko-KOHT) — a term of endearment

kolè (koh-LEH) — anger, fury

konparèt (kon-pah-REHT) — a kind of sweet dry cake from Jérémie, containing coconut and spices, often eaten with fresh avocado

kowosòl (ko-wo-SOHL) — soursop, a large green-skinned, bumpy fruit with creamy, sweet white flesh

Krik? Krak! (kreek? krahk!) — the call-and-answer that begins Haitian folktales and jokes

kriz (kreez) — literally "crisis"; refers to a physical seizure-like condition resulting from grief, emotional shock, etc.

lakou (la-KOO) — A traditional courtyard around which many buildings may be clustered and where extended family members live together, socialize, and pool resources. In rural Haiti, the lakou is also where the dead are buried. The term also refers to the space in which vodou ceremonies take place.

lalo (la-LO) — jute leaves, generally cooked with meat or shellfish and eaten with rice, particularly in the Artibonite region

lam veritab (lahm vay-ree-TAH) — breadfruit

Legba (lehg-bah) — one of the main Vodou spirits, who opens the gates for people to make contact with the other spirits

lòt bò dlo (loht boh dlo) — literally, "the other side of the water"; generally refers to any faraway place where people have gone (particularly, Miami, New York, and other places with large Haitian immigrant populations)

lwa (lwa) — Vodou spirit

machann (mah-SHAHN) — street merchant

Maggi (mah-gee) — Maggi brand bouillon cubes

maladi mistik (mah-lah-DEE mees-TEEK) — a spiritual disease or affliction; a curse

manbo (MAHN-bo) — Vodou priestess

marasa (mah-rah-SAH) — twins; also refers to the twin Marasa spirits in Vodou

maskrèti (mahs-kreh-TEE) — castor oil

mayi moulen (ma-YEE moo-LEHN) — cornmeal porridge

Mezanmi (meh-zahn-MEE) — "Oh my goodness!"

MINUSTAH [*Mission des Nations Unies pour la stabilisation en Haïti*] (mee-nee-STAH) — the UN armed peacekeeping mission, which has been on the ground in Haiti since 2004 and is viewed by many Haitians as an occupation force

monchè (mohn-SHEH) — "my dear," meant affectionately, collegially, or occasionally sardonically

naje pou sòti (nah-JHAY poo soh-TEE) — literally, "swim to escape," a platitude that assumes that one's fate is in one's own control, despite oppressive circumstances

oslè (ohs-LEH) — a game like jacks, played with goat bones

pèpè (peh-PEH) — secondhand clothing and other items, generally sent from North America

pòdyab (poh-JAB) — "poor thing!"

rara (rah-rah) — music and performance of Kanaval (Carnaval) parades, featuring bamboo trumpets and percussion

remèd (reh-MED) — a remedy

restavèk (rest-ah-VEK) — children who are sent to live with others because their families cannot afford to take care of them; in exchange, the children are expected to do household labor—which is sometimes excessive, exploitative, and abusive

salòp (sah-LOHP) — a slob or pig; also sometimes a promiscuous woman

sezisman (say-zees-MAHN) — emotional shock, often understood to be a medical and perhaps spiritual problem

sòs pwa (sohs pwa) — bean sauce, generally eaten with rice or cornmeal porridge

taptap (tahp-tahp) — elaborately painted public bus

tèt chaje (tet chah-JHAY) — literally, "charged or overwhelmed head"—problem, trouble, or affliction; generally used as an exclamation or interjection in the face of any kind of problem or inconvenience, both minor and major

tèt grenn (tet grehn) — kinky-haired

ti granmoun (tee grahn-MOON) — little old person

ti kouri (tee koo-REE) — cornrows

tonmtonm (tohnm-TOHNM) — traditional food of Jérémie and other parts of southern Haiti, made of pounded breadfruit and swallowed with okra sauce

vèvè (veh-VEH) — Vodou symbol usually traced on the ground with chalk powder during ceremonies (and in other contexts as well). Each spirit has his or her corresponding vèvè.

zozo (zo zo) — dick

A Brief History of Haiti

If you have ever seen anything about Haiti on TV or in a newspaper, you probably already have some ideas about what kind of a place it is and what kind of people live there. According to those news stories and fundraising appeals, Haiti is a poor country, populated mostly by dark-skinned people. It is a place of suffering, violence, and disaster. It is a place that needs help.

One problem with those kinds of stories is that they often don't explain how Haiti came to be that way: they depict the suffering, the violence, and the sadness but do not depict the history.

Before independence, Haiti was known as Saint-Domingue, and was a colony of France. Hundreds of thousands of black people, brought to the island from Africa, were enslaved and subjected to unthinkably brutal conditions to produce the sugar that made France very wealthy. So many people died of disease, injury, and overwork that the French had to keep bringing new slaves from Africa every year.

In spite of these conditions, which sought to systematically break their bodies, their minds, their families, and their communities, the enslaved people of Saint-Domingue managed to maintain a sense of identity, community, and self-determination, in part due to the powerful influences of the Creole language and the Vodou religion. Both Creole and Vodou came about because of oppression and loss: torn from their homelands and families, brought to a new world and deprived of basic rights, the ancestors of today's Haitian people formed a new language and a new religion, thus preserving their own humanity and social worlds, and to confront the injustice of their lives. These cultural forms are part of what made the Haitian Revolution possible.

Haiti came into being on January 1, 1804, and it became the first independent black republic, and the only country in history to emerge from a successful, years-long slave rebellion. How remarkable and extraordinary this was cannot be overstated—in 1804, African people and their descendants remained enslaved throughout the Americas. In the United States, slavery would continue for another sixty years.

Much of the rest of the world—particularly the United States and Europe, which still profited hugely from exploited slave labor—refused to recognize the new country of Haiti. The idea of Haiti—of a free black country, a country of slaves who had demanded and fought for their right to be considered human—was economically, socially, and morally threatening to the existing world. And so Haiti was, for the most part, politically ignored and economically stifled.

Over the next two hundred years, Haiti would endure long periods of political instability, increasing socioeconomic inequality, a nearly twenty-year occupation by U.S. Marines, a nearly thirty-year dictatorship, several coups and military juntas, and an unremitting series of foreign military, political, economic, religious, and humanitarian interventions. Historically disadvantaged and often at the whim of more powerful nations, Haiti and its people have struggled for stability, sovereignty, and democracy, while holding on to the memory of the 1804 revolution and the rights and freedom it promised. And, in spite of all this, so many Haitian people retain their sense of community and cooperation, and remain generous, kind, decent, and indisputably, defiantly alive.

It is important to remember that the 2010 earthquake did not occur in isolation. It occurred in a long context of poverty, political strife, and inequality—much of which was produced by Haiti's relationship with other, more powerful countries, including ours.

Suggestions for Further Reading

FICTION

Edwidge Danticat

Breath, Eyes, Memory (1994)

Krik? Krak! (1996)

The Farming of Bones (1998)

Behind the Mountains (2002)

The Dew Breaker (2004)

Brother, I'm Dying (2007)

Marie Vieux-Chauvet

Love, Anger, Madness (1968/2009)

(originally in French, publication suppressed, rereleased in 2005, translated in 2009)

Jacques Stephen Alexis

General Sun, My Brother (1955)

In the Flicker of an Eyelid (1959)

Évelyne Trouillot

The Infamous Rosalie (2003)

NONFICTION

Jonathan Katz
The Big Truck That Went By: How the World Came to Save Haiti and Left Behind a Disaster (2013)

Karen McCarthy Brown
Mama Lola: A Vodou Priestess in Brooklyn (1991)

Paul Farmer
AIDS and Accusation: Haiti and the Geography of Blame (1992)
Haiti After the Earthquake (2011)

Laurent Dubois
Avengers of the New World: The Story of the Haitian Revolution (2004)
Haiti: The Aftershocks of History (2012)

Kathie Klarreich
Madame Dread: A Tale of Love, Vodou, and Civil Strife in Haiti (2005)

SUGGESTED VIEWING

The Agronomist (2004)
Assistance Mortelle (2013)

Acknowledgments

This is a story about kinship—about the people who become part of your world when you least expect it yet most need it. In Haiti, people traditionally live together in homesteads called *lakou*, where they rely on one another, share resources, and form communities. *Hold Tight, Don't Let Go* would not exist without my own community and family, biological and nonbiological alike—without the people who have unstintingly, inconceivably brought me into their lives and become part of mine. Over the past five years, I have received an embarrassment of support, love, and belief from the people who have become my transnational lakou.

Prenel Michel and John Ornélus saved my life on January 12 and demonstrate all that is decent and courageous in ordinary people in a moment of disaster. Martha, Bradley, and Adah King (as well as Ruby Lou, still inchoate) gave me a home to go to when I did not know what the next steps would be; my time as part of their family remains, however unlikely, one of the sweetest periods of my life. Jacques Bartoli, in all his loving tetchiness, always gives me a place to land. Peter Redfield has encouraged my writing in all its forms; his own luminous prose remains a model for me.

Susan Van Metre at Abrams has long left "editor" behind and by now qualifies as "fairy godmother"—having plucked me from obscurity, for reasons that still seem unthinkable to me. Maria Middleton is vying for beatification. Sarah Hepola at *Salon* gave me my first shot. Without Laurent Dubois, none of this would have begun.

It would fill another book to thank everyone as deeply, thoroughly, and individually as I wish to. With gratitude for kindnesses large, small, and larger than they realize, and with apologies for the inadequacy of these words: Sa'ed Atshan, Pooja Bhatia, Jocelyn Chua, Wesline Ciceron, Joëlle Coupaud, Sarah Cussler, Kéthia Édouard, Lauren Fordyce, Jessica Hsu, Josiane Hudicourt-Barnes (a true *manman poul*), Jenn Goheen Golobic and her students, Alicia Gonzalez, Damilove Gorguette, Jenny Greenburg, Saydia Gulrukh, Maryse Jean-Jacques, Besita and Bencille Jeune (without whom my apartment in Port-au-Prince would never have been a home), Kathie Klarreich (for one very necessary kick in the behind), Michel Lafleur, Dragana, Michael, and Jana Lassiter, Mónica, Raúl, Lázaro, and Julieta López, Monica Louis, Alissa Nazaire, Caela O'Connell, Lorien Olive, Erin Parish, Jeremy Popkin, Charles Price, Rachana Rao Umashankar, Fredo "Preciosa" Rivera, Jeannette Acevedo Rivera, Michele Rivkin-Fish, Andrew Ruoss, Merrill Singer, Karla Slocum, Bazelet St. Louis, Silvia Tomášková, Katharine Weber, and Kristien Zenkov. The Rivien and St. Fleur families, and everyone in Degerme, showed incredible generosity and warmth. I am grateful to Cindy Flinn for her unflagging support and candid and enthusiastic feedback on early drafts; I am sorry that she did not see the final version. To the members of the Konbit des Jeunes Penseurs in Port-au-Prince, for your bravery, humor, and heart—no more marvelous inspiration exists in this world.

In her final months, Claudette Wadestrandt did not want to hear about the bad news and sad history from home, but she wanted to hear this story. I read the first complete version aloud over three gray days in January 2012, and she told me it was beautiful and true. She showed me what it meant to yearn for home and that in the end, loving someone means not holding tight but letting go. Christiane "Ti Boum" Mallet Webster, Jacqueline "Kakine" Mallet Cedeno, Marie Florence "Tatou" Wadestrandt, and Olg(uit)a Lasa are proof of the vastness and inclusiveness of family, and of the importance of a good nickname.

Claudine St. Fleur inspires me every day with her bravery and sweetness, and has shown me what it means to have a sister. And finally, to my parents, Arne and Gail Wagner, who have supported me in all endeavors, and have never failed to inspire me to have an encompassing conception of home.

About the Author

LAURA ROSE WAGNER lived in Haiti from 2009 to 2012 and goes back regularly to visit. She, like countless others, survived the January 2010 earthquake through the grace of ordinary people in Port-au-Prince. Laura enjoys learning new languages, connecting with people, making up sonnets and limericks for her friends, eating and talking about Haitian food, and hanging out with her cats, Chouboulout and Djondjon. Her favorite ice cream flavor is coffee. She received a PhD in cultural anthropology in 2014, and is still not 100 percent sure what she's going to be when she grows up. This is her first novel.